TAKE THE NIGHTS BACK

The Lisa Diaries Book 2

LAURA CANNING

Contents

Critical acclaim for Taste the Bright Lights - The Lisa Diaries Book 1	v
Content warning	ix
Belfast, December 2003	xi
1. Gulag	1
2. Room	78
3. Flat	144
Belfast, April 2004	215
Help make a difference	219
Also by Laura Canning	223
About the author	225

Critical acclaim for Taste the Bright Lights - The Lisa Diaries Book 1

"..one of the most authentic teenage voices you'll ever read"

"Outstanding. Breathtaking."

"Canning's writing is that rare thing in the world of books: original and totally honest."

"Exceptional. I was immediately captured by the powerful and witty writing."

"...rings extremely true from the first beat"

"Move over, Ponyboy Curtis. Laura Canning's Taste the Bright Lights does for the twenty-first century teenager what S. E. Hinton's The Outsiders did in the twentieth. The story-line hooks you immediately, leading you into the darkest corners of teenage life. This book deserves the widest possible audience. Read it and then tell others to read it. Brilliant writing."

"... keeps you hooked from start to finish."

"I was totally blown away by this book and read it almost in one sitting."

"The most terrifying book I've ever read. It's scary because it bleeds truth. Incendiary reading. Exemplary writing. I read it in one sitting and couldn't move for an hour afterwards. In fact, I'm still having nightmares about it."

"... Powerful book that took my emotions on a rollercoaster ride. A must read."

"had me laughing one minute and almost crying the next... can't rate it highly enough"

"riveting from the beginning"

"the voice never misses a beat"

"Smart, witty, raw & unique... I couldn't put it down."

"...tragic, sad, infuriating, and very funny - and sometimes all of those at once. A superbly written book."

"one of those books that you can't put down"

"brilliant and compelling... should be on the syllabus of every secondary school"

"This book completely knocked me sideways. It's a page-turner and an eye-opener... speaks for the disenchanted voice of a generation much like 'Catcher in the Rye' would have done to the youth of the 50s."

"Parents!!: READ THIS BOOK! This book screams for you to read it and have long talks with your kids. Read this in one sitting. While it is very dark, there is still hope here. Read it.

Learn from it.

Teach your children from it."

(All reviews on Amazon or Goodreads.)

Content warning

Please be aware that Take the Nights Back contains scenes of violence and sexual violence.

Belfast, December 2003

My ma said I was a silly wee bitch.

My stepda said I was a stupid cunt.

They had the measure of me better than I did.

Gemma says a story should start when something changes. But I don't know when my story – this story – started. It started proper the night I met him, the night we went to the party. But when I think about how I was even there that night, it loops back and back, like pulling in a rope from water. My ma, Paul, even me when I was five.

I don't know.

Really it started with me being stupid. Being a stupid wee bitch.

I'm going to write it I'm going to write it I'm going to write it.

My name's Lisa O'Neill. I'm nineteen and I live in a homeless hostel in Belfast, they brought me here when they let me out of hospital.

I'm here two years now but I can leave any time I want, it's not like the gulag. But I'll stay for a bit, cos I'm waiting for a flat.

I'm going to write what happened when I was fourteen. Maybe it'll help. She says it will.

I have to write it. Cos I want it to stop jabbing at me, slicing at me when something makes me remember. A song that went through my head then and still does now. A man in a red football shirt. A Tesco ham and cheese sandwich. Pink Alberto Balsam shampoo. The stench of drink on breath.

I don't want to remember, but the scenes remember me first and so the footage in my head won't stop.

I'm not mad. She says I'm not, but I know anyway. You just have issues, *she says.*

I do. More issues than a newspaper, *Chrissie and me used to say when the staff said that to us. We'd fall about laughing, then, when I was fourteen.*

Anyway.

I'm putting it off.

This is what happened.

ONE

Gulag

Craigavon, Northern Ireland
April 1999

1.

I didn't fancy him at first. I wouldn't have touched him with a bargepole smothered in tinfoil and then bubblewrapped and attached to another one.

He said his name was Rocky but Rocky my arse, he was like Freddie Mercury in that video hoovering in a dress.

He looked at me. Freddie Mercury. Rocky.

—How old are you? he said, and I said —Fourteen.

He looked at me. He looked at me some more.

He said,

—Do you want some vodka?

So maybe he was all right.

The night I met him and it all started we were in a field sat near on top of a bonfire, trying to keep our wet arses off the damp ground.

We was me and Chrissie, this girl who lived with me in the gulag. The gulag's where I got brought to Be In Care after what the social workers called an Irretrievable Breakdown at home. (The Irretrievable Breakdown was with my ma and my stepda, me and my best mate Nicola ran away and when we got caught my ma said she didn't want me back in the house. Happy fucking days, I thought, cos I didn't want to be in that house either.)

It was a week after Chrissie's birthday, a Friday night, the start of April. You'd think it being April would mean there was a bit more warmth in the air, but there wasn't, it was fucking freezing. So me and Chrissie were sat near on top of the bonfire, trying to keep warm.

The bonfire's where we all went on Friday and Saturday nights, and sometimes Thursdays and Sundays as well if we knew there'd be someone about. *We all* was the four of us from the gulag – me and Chrissie and two fellas our age called Petesy and Darren – and the bonfire was in this field about a mile from the gulag where people not old enough for the pub went to drink. The bonfire was always lit when we got there and there were always loads of people there, at least fifteen or twenty, all around our age or maybe a bit older.

This Friday night when it all started it was just me and Chrissie there from the gulag. Petesy and Darren were away to the offy but me and Chrissie didn't have any money so we went to the bonfire to see if we could scrounge any drink. Sometimes one of the fellas would give us a can of beer or a slug of their Buckfast, if they were a fella who liked us OK cos we'd gone into the other field with them the night or the week before.

We got money for that sometimes too, a tenner usually.

I don't care how that makes me sound. I was only fourteen all these nights at the bonfire, but I already knew shagging was shit and just for fellas, so you might as well get money for it. It meant I could get money to stash away too, cos I was still trying to get to Belfast and away from the gulag and all the social workers.

Anyway, me and Chrissie got a tin of beer off this fella Mark who Chrissie said was all right apart from sticking his tongue down her throat and near choking her when they were in the field the week before. We knocked that beer back fast then we got another two from a fella called Phil who I went with last weekend. He was all right but he'd went on for ages and my bum had got freezing. It was a tenner and a tin he gave me though, so it was all right really.

We arseshuffled even closer to the fire and cracked open our beers. Mark passed us a spliff and then I was warm, tucked beside the fire laughing at everyone's jokes and feeling floaty right away. I love blow even now, if I had the money I'd smoke it all day long.

—Here Chrissie, said this Phil fella, the stud with stamina. —Fancy a wee walk?

Me and Chrissie and everyone else knew *a wee walk* meant *a wee ride*, but Chrissie wasn't scundered at all, she just got up and smirked a bit and followed this fella away from the bonfire and out of the field.

I sat like Dumb and Dumber when she was away, cos I never knew what to say to people and how to talk to them without sounding like a dick, I still don't. But Chrissie was only away about ten minutes, Phil must've been loads faster than he was with me the week before.

I didn't know if that was good or not.

—Right! Chrissie said to me, all bouncy. —C'mon we go to the offy—

And that's how it started.

2.

The man said the party was in the flats. The flats were blocks on the edge of the strip of shops where the off-licence was. They were meant to be dodgy and a girl was meant to have been raped there but we thought that was rumours. We sat on the stairs in them sometimes when it was raining and the bonfire wasn't lit and it was cold. But we hadn't ever been to a proper party in them, in a proper flat, in the warm.

We met the man outside the offy. Me and Chrissie were lurking with intent trying to find someone to go in for us. Chrissie said later it's lucky we didn't find anyone, cos then she would've spent her whole tenner on drink and with what happened next she could keep the tenner for another time.

We bumped into Petesy and Darren beside the offy but Darren wouldn't go in for us even though he never gets asked his date of birth. Chrissie was moaning at him but then she saw the man coming out. He had two bags full of drink so he was a jammy bastard.

—Here, Lisa, ask him, go on—

The man looked at us. He slowed down and looked at us, at me and Chrissie first then all four of us.

Chrissie kicked me to ask him but my words were stuck in my throat. I hated talking to people I didn't know, Chrissie should've done it cos she was a motormouth—

But I didn't ask him, cos he spoke first. He said,

—Here. Do youse want to go to a party?

I wanted to say no at first, that's the thing. He looked like a dick. And he was older, loads older, like thirty or something. He had grey hair at the sides of his head. He had a weaselly face and weaselly wee eyes.

I wanted to say no but I didn't.

—Can we all come, Chrissie said.

The man nodded, looking shocked.

—Course you can! he said. —The more the merrier!

Chrissie snorted when he said *more the merrier* like that. He was definitely a dick. Like someone who wears jumpers, and listens to talking not music on the radio, and drinks things like sherry and – well I don't know, I don't know them types of drinks. But I knew the sort of person. Like social workers.

Chrissie decided it. She always did. We followed the man over to the flats, the four of us. We went inside.

Another time I can't breathe is when I think, what would my life be now, if I didn't go inside.

3.

It was a shite party. We followed this old man up six flights of stairs in dim damp dark. We followed him to a door at the end of a corridor, all peeling paint. 6F, it said on the door.

We followed him through the door, Chrissie first then Petesy then Darren then me. It was a flat and the hallway was dark and the walls were damp. I could smell them. It'd be warm at the bonfire, we could still go back—

But Chrissie decided it again. She stalked after the man into another room, and Petesy and Darren followed her, and then I did too.

It was a living room, smelling of damp like the hall. Another man was there, on a ratty couch. He looked even older than More-the-Merrier and he had on jeans and an Arsenal top and a fleece open over it.

This was shite, two old men and not even a party and 80s music on the CD player for fuck's sake. I thought I'd give it five minutes, to see if any drink showed its face.

Chrissie barged up to the man on the couch. She said,

—Here, I thought this was meant to be a party?

And he said, —Well it is now *you're* here.

He grinned, and now I knew what *leer* meant.

We edged inside, me and Petesy and Darren. Chrissie was already well in, waffling away to these men like she'd known them for yonks. They said their names, More-the-Merrier was Jim and the other fella was Rocky. Chrissie snorted when he said that. Rocky! Freddie Mercury, more like, he had the same teeth.

But he definitely wasn't gay, cos he was gawking at Chrissie as soon as she came in, they both were. Fellas always did gawk at Chrissie. She was fatter than me but she didn't care, at least she didn't seem to from the stuff she wore. This night she was wearing black leggings and a sort of ruffly pink skirt over it, it was gross but at least she was able to wear it.

I was wearing my jeans and black jumper like I always did when we went out, cos even though I still looked ginormous in them the jumper at least covered my arse. Mandy bought me them, she's a foster person I stayed with the couple of days after I got caught by the social workers and the police in Belfast. *You never wear anything nice*, Chrissie had said to me when we were in her room getting ready, *you always just wear jeans and a jumper*. I wanted to say *well jeans and a jumper looks nicer than that Sugar Plum Fairy thing you've got on*, but I didn't cos she'd probably have lamped me.

Chrissie had that skirt on months later, when we saw each other again after I'd run away.

It went up like a rocket when I set it on fire.

Later Chrissie was up dancing with the Jim fella. The songs were still 80s shite but it didn't matter cos we were all getting pissed and stoned. Petesy and Darren were lounging against the walls ignoring the two fellas. I was sat on the arm of the couch, this horrible hairy thing with the Rocky fella (a horrible hairy thing) looking at me.

—How old are you? he said, and I said —Fourteen.

He nodded at me, like he'd thought that or he hadn't thought that or I didn't fucking know anyway. He was only talking to me cos Chrissie was talking to the other fella, he kept looking over at her, sly wee darts of his eyes he thought no-one would notice. I didn't fancy him but it was scundering all the same.

She looked like she was going to cop off here, with this Jim More-the-Merrier fella. She had her arms round his neck and she was singing at him, her beer tin sloshing beside his face. He had his hands on her tits, well not right *on* her tits like HONK, but at the sides letting on he wasn't. But Chrissie didn't seem to mind.

And then they were snogging. I could near see the slabbers of him from where I was sitting—

The Rocky fella looked back at me. I got scundered and put my empty beer tin on the floor so he'd have to look somewhere else for a bit, but even when I was down there I could feel his weasly wee eyes boring into the top of my head. But when I looked up again he said, —Do you want some vodka?

So maybe he was all right.

Later it was better, it was all right.

Freddie Mercury gave me loads of vodka, passing me the big bottle of it even though I was necking loads every time. (I used not to be able not to neck raw vodka but I could by then now, it was easy.) He kept skinning up as well, so I was off my face by then, it was brilliant. Chrissie was whirling around the room to the music and screeching, her pink fluffy skirt flapping out behind her. Maybe she did think she was the Sugar Plum Fairy—

I was on the couch now instead of on the arm of it, talking to Freddie. He was going on about all the fights he'd been in and all the girls he'd shagged (been in) and I was going *yeah?* and *shit*, and *wow*, and eyeing the vodka bottle cos he'd started being tight with it now it was nearly gone.

He still kept looking at Chrissie but she didn't care about anyone now, she was just doing her bouncy wasted thing. More-the-Merrier touched her on the arm a couple of times but she just ignored him.

I was thinking maybe we should head on, cos the vodka was near done and the blow was finished, even the crumbs, and it was boring sitting here listening to this fella.

But still, I wanted him to like me. I don't know why cos I thought he was a bit of a dick, but I think I thought if I sat on for a bit longer maybe he'd snog me yeah right—

But then there was a batter at the front door, someone hammering on it like they were trying to bash it down. Me and Chrissie staggered out for a nosy when More-the-Merrier and Rocky ran out to the door, but they closed it behind them so we saw fuck all.

And I was bored now, and tired, and I had the munchies and there were crisps in my room.

So I couldn't have cared less when More-The-Merrier came back into the living room and said —We should maybe call it a night.

The staff were raging when me and Chrissie got back. We were meant to be in at eleven weekend nights or else the staff had to report us missing to the peelers. They had to sit up waiting for us as well, normally they could go to bed at twelve.

We got in at half three. Joanne and Sean were on that night, they were still in the office. Joanne had bags under her eyes so big you could've used them as binliners.

We stood in the doorway, Chrissie and me. Chrissie did library shoulders, trying not to laugh.

There was some *This is unacceptable*, and *You're putting yourselves at risk* – but we didn't even listen, we just stood there waiting for them to shut up.

—We'll be passing this on to the other staff in the morning, Joanne said, —and discussing your behaviour at the staff meeting on Monday—

Big fucking wow, I thought. If I'd come in at half three, shitfaced, when I was living with my ma and Paul, I'd have been on hospital food for the next week. Here? Big fucking wow.

—Get to bed, Sean said, letting on to be all disgusted, and we did, giggling all the way up the stairs.

4.

I can come home any time I want now, it doesn't matter. I can't be pissed cos the hostel has a no-drink rule – well, I can't be totally pissed and falling over, the staff let on not to notice if people come back only a bit drunk – but I can stay out as late as I want. All night, even.

I tested it a couple of times when I got brought here. I stayed out til four then five then all night, coming back to the hostel at seven in the morning. I stayed behind a bin in an alleyway all night, like me and Nicola did our first night in Belfast. It was cold and it was shite and I was freezing even with my cider, but I wanted to see. But all that happened was one of the staff saying God Lisa, you had us worried, *and,* You don't have to, but if you're staying out maybe ring and let us know—

It was Gemma who said that. She's the deputy manager in the hostel here. She's all right. She's the one said to write my story down, to see if it'll help.

(I'll never ring the hostel. I've no phone. I'll never have a phone again.)

I don't mind the hostel really, though I'd never say it (it'd be like saying you like school dinners). I hate it sometimes. Not the hostel, not really, but the walls close in and I can't breathe. Sometimes wanting my own flat hits me so hard the thought's like a bucket of water in the face. Sometimes I think I can't be in this place, any place that's not mine, even another minute.

I've been in this room here, on the top floor, nearly two years. It was a dump when I first saw it, all bare. The walls are a sort of damp grey and the paint peels off in some bits and the chest of drawers is all scratched, but it looks a bit better now I've been here for ages. You can't polish a shite, course you can't, but you can cover it up a bit.

It looks all right, my room. For what it is. I'm not allowed my own duvet cover cos of health and safety and A Possible Fire Risk, but I've got a red sort of satin curtain I got in a charity shop for a quid and I have that over the bed. I have a lamp, a yellow one cos I like yellow. And cos I can't see a bare bulb from a ceiling now, cos of all the times I stared up at it in the B&B.

We're not meant to make food in our rooms, cos of health and safety again, but I've got a kettle in mine, hidden in the wardrobe and under clothes cos the staff do room checks every Sunday. I've got a big plastic box with a lid too, I keep food in it. I don't have to hide it cos everyone keeps food in their rooms otherwise it'd get nuck. I've got teabags and coffee and Coffee Mate and bread and cornflakes and Cup a Soup and Pot Noodles, and a bowl and mug I got from the charity shop.

I want my own place so much it cry sometimes, like properly cry. It's like a band going round my chest when I imagine it, it's hard to breathe. But it'll be ages before I get a flat, cos I have to wait for one on from the Housing Executive. I can't save for a private rental cos I can't get a job, cos I get a job I don't get benefits, so my hostel rent's not funded so then I have to leave. And I can't sleep out again.

I know how to get money.

But I can't, again.

5.

I grabbed the vodka off Freddie Mercury.

—Gimme that, I said.

I swigged, as much as I could. I was hyped up, pissed off, ready to get wasted and punch walls.

I'd seen my ma and Paul earlier, at the shopping centre.

I swigged at the bottle again, deep and deep, til the roaring in my head and ears muffled.

Chrissie had knocked on my door earlier that day, about twelve. I hadn't been arsed going down for breakfast so I was lying in bed eating crisps and watching telly and chilling. I hadn't even been arsed getting dressed. I was dying for a tin of Coke cos I was thirsty from all the vodka the night before but there was a sink in my room so I had some stinking water from that.

Chrissie wanted me to go to Rushmere with her. Rushmere was the big shopping centre a couple of miles from the gulag and we went there loads at weekends cos there was fuck all else to do.

I said OK, cos there was fuck all else to do and cos it was easier to say OK to Chrissie than tell her no.

And then we saw my ma and Paul.

It was in the shopping centre and we were lurking with intent outside an offy again, cos Chrissie wanted to see if she could nick a bottle of vodka so she didn't have to spend the tenner from Phil on drink for later. There was no chance of course, they wouldn't even have let us set foot in the offy and even if we did the spirits and the Buckfast were all security tagged and Chrissie could hardly stick a crate of beer inside her coat.

But we kept dandering past, cos Chrissie said there might be a minute when the staff person was out the back getting stock or something and we could run in, lift something and then run out of the shopping centre before they caught us. Her and Darren did it a few months ago, she said, she was probably still on the CCTV.

Yeah right, I was about to say, joking, and then I looked round and there was my ma and Paul and the two devil children Anthony and Ryan.

They were hardly any distance away from us, a few trolleys' worth. They were looking right at me, Paul beside my ma with his hand on one of the devil children's shoulders, like he was posing for a family portrait or something. The Addams Family, ha ha.

My stomach clenched and squirted, so hard they must've seen it in my face. Now they'd think I was scared of them and I wasn't, it was just seeing them, him, like that when I wasn't expecting it. I must've looked like what our form teacher used to call *a slack-jawed Neanderthal*, gaping over at them.

Then I was able to be me again and I gave them all a dirty look.

My ma was wearing that stinking purple leopardskin coat that made her look like Kat off Eastenders, and she'd so much makeup on you'd near have had to chisel it off. The devil children were just the devil children, all dirt and snot. And Paul – Paul looked smaller. He was only about Petsey's size, I'd never noticed before he was small. Small Paul. Heh.

I kept giving them a dirty look, cos I wasn't going to be the one to look away first. It was like a Western, a standoff outside Winemark.

Chrissie noticed.

—Here, is that your ma? she said, loud, too loud like she always did when she wanted to scunder someone. —And your stepda, what do you call him, Paul? Is that PAUL?

I could see Paul's face start to darken and I near took a step back, I couldn't help it. But part of me was hoping he'd go for it, he'd kick off here in Rushmere and lamp Chrissie and it would all be on CCTV and he'd get done for it cos me and Chrissie – the Injured Parties – we were In Care now so someone would have to do something about it.

The devil children started up now too, all *There's Lisa! Dad, that's Lisa!* and I didn't know what was going to happen.

But my ma… my ma just stood there. She didn't look sundered or ashamed or like she missed her daughter who was in care cos of her and her psycho husband. She even glared a bit.

Chrissie said again,

—Is it, but? Is that your ma and HIM?

It only lasted a couple of seconds. And I didn't know what to do, how I should react, should I shout and scream at them or try and hit him or turn on my heel and stalk away or what? It was like it was all up to him and I had to just wait to see what he was going to do.

But then Paul grabbed my ma by the elbow and he said to them all, —Come on, and then, —Come ON! when it looked like the devil children weren't going to move cos they wanted to see blood and broken teeth.

And then they were gone, them and their trolley swallowed up among the shoppers.

I stood there glaring after them for a bit cos it was the only thing I could do, then I caught on I probably looked like a mentalist so I stopped. I looked at Chrissie. She had that bright look in her eyes I hated.

She said,

—Why'd you not say nothing, I'd have said something, I'd have told them all to fuck away off—

And I said it was cos I couldn't be bothered, that they weren't worth it.

So when Chrissie said later Jim had texted and said did me and her want to go to the flat later to meet her and Rocky, I thought fuck yeah.

Freddie Mercury took the vodka back off me.

—Cheer up it'll never happen, he said, and I nearly snarled *what the fuck do you know*.

But it was his mate's flat, again. And they had drink and blow, again. So I twisted my face into a sort of smile.

—There you are, he said.

He patted my thigh.

He slid over to me.

—Go on, he said. —Have more if you want—

Fuck it. I didn't care. I grabbed the vodka back off him.

—Gimme that, I said, and I swigged it again, as much as I could manage in one go and then I choked on it. My eyes watered and there was roaring in my ears and under it I could hear Chrissie jeering at me. —You drink like a kid, she said, —dress like a granny and drink like a kid—

Freddie Mercury and More-the-Merrier laughed. I hated them.

But then Freddie put his arm round me. And I let him, cos my eyes were tight like I was going to cry.

Chrissie laughed again.

—Fuck off, Chrissie! I snapped at her. It was fucking thick of me cos she'd destroy me in the gulag if we fell out, and I was starting at her school that Monday too. But I didn't give a shit. Not that night.

She saw it in my eyes.

—Oooooooh! she went, pretending I was joking. But she glared.

There was nearly another standoff, but More-the-Merrier grabbed her, one arm rough around her waist. He pulled her to him.

—C'mon now, girls, don't be fighting, he said. —We're here to have a laugh—

And Chrissie said, —Well stop bogarting the vodka then Lisa, you greedy bitch— and we all laughed and I passed over the bottle.

—It's cos her stepda's a bastard, Chrissie said later, low and hushed like telling secrets.

Me and Rocky were on the couch and she was on the floor with Jim. There was music on, shite techno but at least it was music and there'd been blow so my foot started to tap a bit.

But, Paul. His face wouldn't leave my head. I'd thought for months what I'd do if I saw him, and now I'd fucked it up.

Jim and Rocky tried to take me out of it. They said stuff like, *Well what did you get up to today, Lisa?* And, *How do you two know each other?* And I knew that last one was shite, cos Chrissie had told Jim about the gulag the night before.

But they tried. Well, Jim and Rocky did. Chrissie rolled her eyes when I kept saying things like *Nothing* and *Just*.

And then she said that about Paul.

—I thought you… didn't live with him, Rocky said, pretending he didn't know I lived in the gulag.

—She doesn't, Chrissie said, again with that hushed voice like telling a kid a bedtime story. —But her ma and her stepda live in Craigavon and we saw them today—

I wanted to tell her to fuck up, but I'd never get away having a go twice in one night. I was already lucky she hadn't lamped me. But she needed to shut the fuck up. I forgot about Paul. I didn't know these two fellas and here Chrissie was telling them my business—

But Rocky put his arm around me again.

And he said,

—Is he a real bastard, like?

And I nodded my head a bit yeah.

—What'd he do, Rocky said, —did he—

He meant had Paul been at me the way Chrissie's da had been at her.

I couldn't having them, anyone, thinking that.

So I said it. It was the first time I'd said it to anyone, the first time I'd said it out loud. I hadn't told Nicola, even, and she was my best mate for years. But it was easier somehow, with this man's arm around me, and his face creased up all concerned.

I said,

—He used to hit me, that's all—

—Ach Lisa, Rocky said. He pulled me in even closer. He stroked my hair and it was so nice I nearly cried.

I held onto him.

—Hitting you all the time, like? he said, and I said yeah.

He tutted. He stroked my hair again. I let him.

Chrissie wasn't getting any attention. So she said,

—Well! That's nothing compared to what *my* da did to *me*!

Jim said, —What? And she came out with it.

She said it the exact same as that first night we were out together, at the bonfire a couple of weeks ago. She'd probably told so many people it just came out. I bet she could tell about it in her sleep.

I looked at her, spilling everything. I didn't know how she did it, cos I'd be so scundered, mortified, I couldn't even say it. It was bad enough saying Paul hit me.

But Jim and Rocky listened like they were on Jerry Springer. Chrissie loved it.

—So I says to her, What about all the other times he was in my bed, you didn't say nothing about it then, and she says to me, You're a lying wee bitch!

She looked round at all of us when she said *lying wee bitch*, a script would've said Dramatic pause. It was the exact place she stopped at before. And like me Jim said, shocked and on cue, —What?

—Aye, Chrissie said, —lying wee bitch she called me! So I ended up telling the counsellor at school about it, but my ma still said I was lying, so she kicked me out of the house—

She did another Dramatic Pause, so Jim and Rocky could tut and gasp. I didn't bother. I'd heard it before.

But then she said,

—Lisa's ma kicked her out as well, didn't she Lisa?

And then we talked about me, and I don't know why but I wasn't all hot-faced and heart thumping like usual – well, not too much. I told them about the squat in Belfast and then getting caught. And how my ma didn't want me back, so now I was In Care.

We talked fast then, all of us saying stuff. We talked about shitty mas and das, and stupid teachers, and dickhead social workers not having a clue.

Rocky had been in a home when he was fourteen too. He'd been in jail later as well, cos he found his da after and beat him up so bad his da was in intensive care for a week.

—Good, I said, and he laughed and hugged me and said I was a wee warrior.

I snuggled into him.

Jim's ma was an alco. There was never food in the house so he'd nick it, and he got caught and sent to Hydebank when he was fifteen.

Then here was blow and another bottle of vodka. We drank and smoked and talked, til I was loads better. Not like huggy group therapy, like the Exploring Issues they tried in the gulag. Jim and Rocky knew what'd happened to us. They'd lived it, not just read it in books. They didn't just pretend to be interested either, like the social workers. They were nice.

They listened to us. They knew.

Chrissie and Jim were wrapped up together. Chrissie leaned against him and he wrapped his arms round her tight. He kissed her neck.

I looked at Rocky, properly, for the first time.

I didn't want to shag him I didn't think. Maybe if he wanted to, cos it was brilliant having the flat instead of drinking outside, but I didn't really want to. I was there for booze and blow.

But he was all right really, when I looked at him this night. He had Freddie Mercury's teeth, and loads of tiny white spots around his mouth, but he had big brown eyes, all soft and concerned since I'd said about Paul. Maybe he was all right—

He was a mind reader, cos he leaned into me.

He kissed me, very gently.

He wasn't like fellas my own age, who launch when you're halfway through saying something and stick their tongues down your throat like they're trying to choke you.

It was gentle. I'd never had gentle.

I kissed him back.

He put his hand on my face. He pulled me to him. It sounds rough but it wasn't, it was lovely. He stroked my hair. He stroked my face. He smiled, and stroked my hair again.

—YEEOOOW! Chrissie shouted.

Her and Jim smirked. Not a bad smirk, a slagging one, teasing. It was nice. Rocky smirked as well but that was nice too. It was good, this. It was far better than being pissed off at my ma and Paul—

—I think we're surplus to requirements, Chrissie said to Jim. I was about to say *fucking hell Chrissie where'd you get that dictionary you swallowed*, but her and Jim were out of the room, giggling and squealing like an aftershave ad. Feet ran upstairs, then a door slammed.

Then nothing, just the music.

I wouldn't look at him. I don't know why. But he took my chin and tilted it up, again gently.

—Now, he said. —Where were we?

6.

He only snogged me that night, but Chrissie shagged Jim.

She told me the next day, when we were behind the bins outside the gulag having a spliff she'd scrounged off him after.

I wasn't really listening. Not cos Chrissie was boring the tits off me – even though she was – but because it was Sunday now and I had to start my new school the next day. Kate Kruger my social worker (she was called Kate Kruger cos when she remembered to try and do a smile she looked like the murderer from Nightmare on Elm Street) had told the gulag staff to remind me.

When Chrissie shut up about Jim I said I wasn't going to school the next day.

I shouldn't have said anything, cos Chrissie was the sort of person who listened all sympathetically to something you were bothered about then threw it in your face the next day. But I couldn't help it.

—You'll have to, Chrissie said. —Or they might stick you in Alcatraz—

Alcatraz was this place near Belfast, Madison House, Chrissie had told me about before. It was where social workers put under-sixteens In Care who they decided were Out of Control. Inmates didn't out get to for school, even, cos there was a school there and teachers came in every day, and no-one got to go out except to town maybe once a month and only then with staff. And once you were put there you were there til you were sixteen.

I didn't know when she told me the first time and I didn't now that Sunday whether Chrissie was taking the piss about Alcatraz or not. Whether I'd get put there just for saying I didn't want to go to school. When we'd smashed my ma's windows and got lifted by the peelers a few weeks before, Chrissie had said then that social workers couldn't do anything to us, not really—

Chrissie did go to school, though. Mostly—

So I didn't know.

But that was the thing about Chrissie and why she'd never be my best mate the way Nicola had been, cos I never knew if she was just winding me up just for the sake of it, just to be a bitch. Nicola never did that. We'd taken the piss out of each other all the time, but it was just slagging, mucking about, we didn't try and make the other one feel bad just because.

I got a big wave of missing Nicola, missing all of them, and I took a big draw on the spliff to hide it.

I said,

—They're not going to put me in Alcatraz just cos I don't go to school—

Chrissie looked at me. She shrugged.

—Just saying, she said. —No skin off my nose either way—

Sometimes I hated her. Like really hated her.

But I was scared of her a bit, cos if I fell out with her then she'd get Petsey and Darren and the other fella in the gulag, Tommy, against me. And things would be worse than when me and Nicola fell out a few months before that, when I was still living with my ma and Paul. At least when I fell out with Nicola I could get away from her and everyone at school at home time, even if I did have to go home to my ma and Paul. People from school couldn't follow me home or come into my room or anything.

But Chrissie could let the fellas into the girls' cluster at night if she wanted, or try and break the door in with them when I was in the bath like she'd done before. I wanted to stay on side with Chrissie. She knew it too I think, the bitch.

Lying in bed that night I thought again about not going to this new school. Just saying I wasn't going, being all rebel without a school and *over my dead body*. But Chrissie had sort of scared me about Alcatraz. So when Joanne came and woke on the Monday morning, I thought maybe I should get up even if I was still a bit spaced still from Saturday night at Rocky's. But I nearly cried at the thought of it, and then I did cry a bit.

I didn't have a uniform cos Joanne was going to take me into town after school to get one, so I put on my jeans and black jumper again. The jumper smelled of smoke and blow and maybe BO so I sprayed deodorant all over it then there was all white marks I had to try and get off with my facecloth wet in the sink.

Joanne gave the jumper a look when I came down the stairs to the dining room, but she didn't say anything. Chrissie and Petesy and Darren were already in the dining room, and Tommy as well but sitting on his own like always. No-one bothered him about it either, cos he just didn't care. Chrissie always called him a weirdo. I let on to agree, but really I wanted to ask him how he did it, just not care.

It was porridge for breakfast, and Chrissie took the piss cos I was going into school/jail that morning, but she was only joking, I didn't mind. I tried to spin breakfast out a bit, getting more toast even though I was stuffed, but then Joanne said, —Right, everyone ready? And we all went out and got into the minibus. There was a fight about seats but I didn't care, I just wanted to be there and the day to be over and then the next ones and then I'd be sixteen.

I didn't know the school cos it was about ten miles from my last one so it wasn't one of the ones we used to fight with. —Good luck, Joanne said, giving me three quid for my lunch and then this schoolbag she'd bought for me, all shiny and new with jangling straps. I didn't look in it. I held it and I followed Chrissie up the drive. I wanted to run.

It was all right, in the end. Well, not all right, cos I was scundered all day with everyone looking at me and wondering who I was and why I wasn't wearing a uniform, but it wasn't as bad as it could've been. Chrissie took me down to the office and I had to go in and see the head teacher, a woman with a moustache called Mizz McGee. She was all right. She said all the usual stuff about being very pleased to see me and she hoped I'd be very happy and to come and see her or talk to my form teacher if I had any problems any at all. But she was all right.

—Well, she said after ages of going on and I was starting to be sure I could smell my jumper cos her office was so warm, —I'll leave you in Chrissie's capable hands then, and remember to come and see me if you have any problems any at all—

I knew I never would.

I thought about Nicola a lot that day. Chrissie sort of ignored me in school, she went straight over to a crowd in our form room and didn't even say *this is Lisa*, or anything. She was probably only mates with me in the gulag cos we were the only girls. And I thought, me and Nicola were meant to be best mates, but she'd only come to see me once. So maybe we hadn't been best mates at all—

And then I thought, maybe Nicola had looked down on me a bit, not really meaning to, but feeling sorry for me cos she had the nice ma and da and she was nice looking and everyone liked her. Everyone liked her better.

But there was Rocky now. He liked me. Maybe he liked Chrissie first and he only talked to me cos Chrissie got together with Jim – but I thought he did like me now after I said about my ma and Paul. His da used to hit him too, and he'd been in a home, we were the same. I thought I'd maybe talk to him about Nicola. See what he said.

Joanne came to get me early, to get my new uniform. She got me two skirts and they were a size 14 and the jumpers she got were a 16. *It's just a number on a label*, she said when she saw my face, but that was easy for her to say cos the number on her label mustn't be any higher than 8.

7.

By Wednesday that first week of school I was going nuts, I'd had enough. I wanted to get pissed and stoned.

—Here, do you have Jim's number? I said to Chrissie, after Joanne dropped us back at the gulag and me and Chrissie were out by the bins again having a smoke.

—What for? she said, cos she was nosy and couldn't help herself.

—Just, I said, —I was thinking of maybe heading round there—

Chrissie crowed.

—You want to see Rocky! she said, all triumphant like she'd won a bet.

I didn't really, I just wanted drink and blow. But I really wanted drink and blow, so I let her think whatever she wanted.

—I'll text him, she said, and within five minutes there was a text back telling us to call round.

It was just the four of us again, me and Chrissie and Jim and Rocky. As soon as we got there Jim grabbed Chrissie by the hand and pulled her up the stairs. So it was just going to be me and Rocky and I was nervous now cos I'd snogged him the last time, he'd probably expect more now and he had the drink.

We sat on the hairy couch together. He lit up a spliff.

—I missed you, he said.

I didn't know what to say.

—What've you been up to, he said.

I wasn't going to but then I did. I smoked the rest of the spliff and I said about school and being on my own, and maybe Nicola from my old school hadn't ever been my friend. I mean, I know she was, sort of was, but not the way I'd been friends with her. Not now I was thinking about it.

—Fuck her, he said, —what're you worrying about her for when you don't even see her?

He was right maybe. Nicola and that school and my ma and Paul were years ago it felt like, and now there was Chrissie and the new school and the home and everything was different. And there was Rocky now too, maybe.

—You can come round any time, you know, he said. —If stuff's pissing you off. Just text me and you can come round here or we can go to mine and talk—

—I've no phone, I said, clenching my toes inside my shoes. Who didn't have a phone even back then, nearly everyone had one by then.

—What! he said.

I sat there, looking at the floor. My face burned, I could feel it.

He put his fingers under my chin and lifted my face up.

—Well, he said, —we'll just have to sort that out, won't we?

8.

Jim's flat was a dump and so was Rocky's when I saw it later but I didn't care, I'd have loved even a stinking place like that back then and I'd love one now. I don't care.

I don't know where my flat's going to be if I ever get one. I'm on the list for a one-bedroom but there's hardly any of them cos of Family Priority and Housing Need. A house would be brilliant, I'd nearly faint in shock if they gave me one but I know they won't.

I've got three Areas of Choice, on the housing list. I walk around their streets a lot like a King Billy No Mates. Sun, snow, storms, pissing rain, I walk in all of them. I'd be on someone's Neighbourhood

Watch list except around here that's the RA or the UVF and I don't think they've got a list, not that sort anyway.

Most of the houses are dumps, they've got rubbish all over the paths and kids like you see on the news when there's rioting. But a couple of streets are all right looking and a couple of the houses look all right too. Like my ma's in Craigavon. Our estate was a bit of a dump but our house was all right cos my ma would've cracked up if it didn't look nice for the neighbours. (She had a rockery in the front garden for fuck's sake. A rockery! I used stones from it to break her windows.)

Merley Street's the best one, in the streets in my three Areas of Choice. It's got two rows of tidy houses and all the houses have titchy paved gardens about the size of a double bed. The houses are titchy too, but there's something about them, they look like homes. There's Christmas lights up in some of them already. I might do Christmas lights if I ever get my own place.

The best house in Merley Street's at the end, cos sometimes the dog's in the garden. He's a black lab, a puppy, and he knows me now so if he's in the garden he goes mental, jumping up to lick my hand through the gate. His arse goes from side to side like the tail on a clock. I want to nick him but I can't. I wouldn't anyway, cos then he'd be sad.

If I get a house not a flat it'd have a hallway all lit by soft lamps like I saw on telly once, and it'd be warm when I came home. I'd have a dog as well. He'd be with me all the time, but when I think about this hallway the dog's waiting on me getting back He bounces over to me like I'm the best thing in the world. And later we do the Christmas decorations, him and me. I put tinsel on his collar.

I'm putting it off again, I know I am. I need to say about Rocky.

9.

Later the vodka was done and the ashtray was full of blow butts and I was off my face the way I wanted.

Rocky put music on. I couldn't follow it. I kept forgetting it was on, I kept going in and out of it. Like a dream.

He rolled another spliff.

The music was slower and I think the vodka was finished but had we even had any, maybe it was yesterday, or some other time, I didn't know. I lay on the couch and he sat on the floor.

He shifted closer. He stroked my leg. The strokes were to the rhythm of the music and I drifted back into it.

His hand went up further. He rubbed at me, between my legs. It was harder than the leg stroking and I came out of the music. I sat up.

—Ssssh, he said, and helped me lie back down. He was gentle again. I drifted again.

His hand was inside my jeans. He snapped the button open and eased the zip down. He rubbed again, over my knickers. It was gentle so I let him. It was nice. I moved my hips a bit to the music. It was nice.

His hand moved to the top of my knickers. It snaked inside. It pushed my knickers down. Not right down, enough to get in, but I didn't want him to. I wanted to lie here and chill. I sat up again, out of my drift.

—Ssssh, he said again, taking my shoulders and pushing me down, and after a bit I started to drift to the music again and he put first one and then two fingers inside me.

When he tugged my jeans and then my knickers off he'd been rubbing and fingering for ages, forever, so I let him. He'd shag me now. He could. I'd look like a dick saying no now—

And I'd been smoking his blow and drinking his vodka all night, so I sort of knew it was coming. I wasn't scared, cos I'd done it loads even only with fellas my own age. But I wasn't turned on either, not like you see women on TV gasping and going *Oh oh oh*. I never had been. Shagging's just something you do, you sort of have to—

It was like watching myself through glass.

He climbed onto the couch. He got over me. He lowered himself down. He nudged with his knee to push my legs apart. I pulled them back together. I thought I wasn't scared, but I couldn't help it.

He pushed with his knee again and his dick pushed at me. I squirmed a bit.

I think writing this now I hoped he'd change his mind. Cos I didn't really want to, not really, but I couldn't stop by then or else I'd be a prick tease.

But he took my legs and he held my knees up and he shoved into me. Oh it was sore it was sore it was sore. It hurt before sometimes but never like this, was it cos he was older—

I screamed. But only a bit, cos I didn't want Chrissie to hear.

—You're ready, he said, —I got you ready, it can't be sore—

He pushed in again. Oh it was sore it was sore it was sore. The music went on, but I wasn't drifting now and my heart was screaming in my ears. He panted on me, there was vodka and smoke on his breath. His hip bones dug into my thighs. He went faster.

I was scared to look frigid and like a kid. I had to do it right. I moved under him. I moaned a bit. The music went on and I thought to its rhythm *hurry up hurry up hurry up*.

He did a sort of moan then he collapsed on top of me. I lay under him, tense and freaked. I didn't know what to do. I'd never had a fella lie on me like this after, they pulled up their jeans and their kaks and away they went. Could I, should I, push him off?

Then there was wet *stuff*, him, running out of me, and all of a sudden I was nearly crying.

I shifted under him. He got the hint and pushed himself off me. I drew my legs back and tried to sit up, but the *stuff* was all over the couch.

I looked for my knickers. They were pooled inside my jeans, scrumpled on the floor. I snatched at them, fast cos he was watching me and my face was burning.

I swung my legs round. I tried to get my knickers on. It felt like there was bucketloads coming out of me, bucketloads of *stuff*, and as I pulled my knickers on I saw brown blood streaked on my thighs.

I looked at the couch. He watched me. He said,

—You've made a right mess of that haven't you!

All cheerful! It's only a saying, but seriously I didn't know where to look. I was scundered, mortified.

—Sorry, I said.

There was a thump from upstairs, a door slamming, and laughing on the stairs. Chrissie and Jim were coming down—

I yanked my knickers up, fast fast.

I was pulling my jeans up when the living room door opened. Chrissie saw everything in a fast glance, the way she did. She laughed.

She said,

—What've you two been up to?

We were late back to the gulag again. Only one o'clock this time but the staff were still raging cos it was a school night and cos of us being in at half three the Saturday before. It was David and Sinead on, I thought David was going to hit us. The vodka was wearing off and I was shivering and I just wanted to go to bed. And I was still sore, and I felt all slimy and gross and I wanted a bath.

They let us go eventually. Chrissie and me hauled ourselves up the stairs, hanging on to the bannister and climbing up like the stairs were a mountain. I wondered what Jim had done to her, if she was as sore as me.

When I got into my room and locked the door behind me I couldn't be bothered even having a wash never mind a bath. I just wiped myself with my knickers and threw the knickers on the floor, and got into my jammies and got into bed.

. . .

10.

I had my last bath about a month after that. It was in the B&B in Belfast. That makes me sound like a minging bitch, but I wash and have showers course I do, I just can't have baths anymore. I was happy in my last bath, I was the happiest I'd been in ages. Til I got out.

There's a bath just down the corridor here in the hostel but I've never used it. The bit of the hostel I'm in has the bathroom and a toilet at one end, then two rooms then mine. Fellas live in the two rooms but they don't hassle me any more, they've given up.

I don't want a bath in my new flat. I probably won't have one anyway cos it'll be a tiny wee place, but if there's one there I'll put stuff in it. Clothes or boxes or books even, but I don't have any books. Plants maybe. I could fill the bath up with dirt and plant stuff in it. I won't be getting in.

11.

The next time I saw Rocky it was a bit better, he was gentler. It was still sore when he shoved in at the start, but I knew it wouldn't last long and anyway I was a bit pissed by then. And he'd been good to me, really good to me listening about the gulag and Nicola. So it didn't — shouldn't — matter.

He got up to get more drink from the kitchen. I swooped at my chance like a ninja and I got the *stuff* wiped up with my knickers. I pushed them deep into my jacket pocket to rinse them out later.

I wasn't going to lie there flashing my arse over the place, so I went to pull my jeans on. But he came back and said
—Aw, don't get dressed yet—

So I didn't. But I couldn't lie there in the nip like some poser, so I said I was cold so he'd get his sleeping bag. We lay under it. The material was cold and slippery on my arse.

He spooned me. It was all right for about ten seconds then he started twisting at my tit. I didn't like it, cos it was a bit sore and cos I didn't want to shag again. But I wanted to stay there warm and cuddled, so I didn't say anything.

He said,

—Fancy coming to mine on Friday, instead of here? Next block over, 10D—

—What about Chrissie, I said.

He laughed.

—Sure her and Jim are love's young dream, they'll probably be glad to get the place to themselves—

I was scared then to be in their way, so I said all right.

—You're great, he said.

He kissed my neck.

I snuggled into him, cos it was nice to be held and cos he'd finally let go of my tit. He kissed my neck again.

—So Friday? he said. —After school?

I said yeah.

—You're class, he said again, holding me tight.

That was the first time. When I thought yeah, maybe I can trust you, maybe there's someone on my side at last.

. . .

12.

I'm in work today. Well, New Deal.

I work in a Spar. It's cos of Learning Life Skills and Learning about the Workplace, the dole make me go. I've been here two months so I've another four months to do. There's meant to be training one day a week but no-one's sorted it yet and the dole said to start at the shop anyway, cos if I didn't they wouldn't process my payments.

I get forty quid a week for New Deal. It's shite, even the hostel staff knows it is, but I have to do it to keep my dole cos if I lose my benefits I'm fucked, out of the hostel and back on the streets.

It's two buses and an hour and a half travel each way to the Spar, five days a week, Monday to Friday, early and late shifts To Be Arranged Weekly. I can't be even five minutes late or I'll get sanctioned. I'm scared to take a sick day, even. (I did once and Gemma rang them. I was dying with a hangover but I told Gemma I'd my period, so she said to the dole I was indisposed. *They got all arsey and said I needed a sick note, but Gemma got arsey back and said how could someone get a sick note for period pains, were they meant to call the doctor out one day every month—*

Like I said, Gemma's all right. We talk sometimes. I told her that time, later, I said I'd a hangover and it wasn't my period, but she just laughed and said sure we've all been there. *She knows I'm writing my story down and she says it might be good for me, to Come to Terms. But she can't read it. This is only for me.*

Anyway, I'm in the Spar today, doing my slave labour. The Spar's in the south part of Belfast, near the university. The streets are nicer there. I don't know how exactly, but they're wider and they've got trees and no-one jeers. Maybe if I'd grew up round here I'd never have been in the gulag, but then I think Paul would've been a cunt wherever we lived.

When the Housing Executive asked me for my Areas of Choice, a year and a half back, I said south Belfast, around the university. I heard somewhere this was an OK place to live, maybe in the days I was sleeping outside. The woman in the Housing Executive laughed at me. You'll be waiting years, *she said. I checked with people in the hostel and she was right. Five years at least, they said. Maybe ten.*

But I'm going to move here sometime, someday. When I've got money and a proper job and more than forty quid a week for it. I'll have loads of money and a nice house and maybe even swishy hair and clothes that's not tracksuits. Never high heels, but, cos I'll never wear them again.

I need the money and the job first though.

When I had to do New Deal I thought forty quid a week was loads, I started saving from it for a deposit on a private rental. But after a month of really trying I only had eighteen quid and I cried so then I drank it.

I'll start my jobs off in a pub, I think, cos jobs there aren't too hard to get – at least, I think they're not. And it'll be a nice pub cos it's over this side of the city, not like the ones with barbed wire outside that's near the hostel. There'll be lots of laughing in this pub, and there'll be regulars as well and they'll come in and say how's Lisa.

There's two thoughts in my head I like, that I don't push down right away. The first one's the dog in my own house and doing the Christmas decorations, that's my favourite. The other one's this pub and me behind the bar, cos I've a job there.

The dog thought is a video, like a home movie, where he runs out to meet me when I come home. But the pub one's like an old photo. It's an old-fashioned pub, not all shiny and chrome. The picture in my head is me behind the bar, pulling a pint and laughing cos I'm messing about with one of the regulars. He's a fella, but it's nothing dodgy, nothing bad. I'm wearing makeup as well. I don't look ugly.

If I could get work somewhere, three or four months' worth, cash in hand after New Deal, I could get a private rental. Only a room in a shared place, but I could get a proper job then and save up for my own place. It'd be about three hundred quid for a deposit and the first month's rent in a shared house, to start me off.

I think about it all the time, I'm obsessed. It's like a bluebottle round a bulb how much it's in my head, how can I get three hundred quid how.

I'm working with Niall today. He's a student with sideburns and spots who lives in the next street, he's all right. He goes all scundered sometimes when he talks to me, so I used to think maybe he fancies me. He probably doesn't, he probably thinks I'm a bit of a slut and maybe I'll let him shag me, so he thinks he fancies me cos of that. (He wouldn't know he thinks that, but I bet that's it.)

Niall's not on New Deal so he gets a proper wage from the shop cos it's a proper job cos he's not on benefits. He always says he's skint, but he's talking shite cos he smokes proper cigarettes and not rollies like me. When he goes for a smoke he always says to me do you fancy one too, *and I always say take one. But it's a teeny shop so there's only ever the two of us on, so if anyone comes in he drops his smoke real fast and rushes in. He's a bit of an old woman cos he's the senior staff. But he's all right.*

Friday's always a late day. The shop's open til ten and I have to stay til then on Fridays and one other night To Be Confirmed Weekly. Niall says to me,

—*Are you heading out after work?*

Him and the students and most of the other ones who come into the shop talk different than me. Slower. Like the staff at the hostel. Like, not in a rush to get words out. Like, people will wait for them. They say their words properly too, sort of softer.

Maybe I'd be like that if I was a student. If I'd stayed at school past the gulag and done my GCSEs and my A levels and had a ma and da who wanted me to. Sometimes I think I should go back, but mostly I can't be arsed.

Maybe Nicola's at the university, I think sometimes. If she'll come into the shop, cos the university's only up the road. I don't know. I haven't seen her since she came to the gulag just after I got there. I thought about ringing her old number once, her ma and da's house one in Craigavon, and asking if she had a mobile number. Gemma would let me use the office phone. But I didn't.

Niall's got this hopeful face on him, waiting for me to answer him. He looks like a puppy.

I tell him no.

I don't know why he keeps asking, cos I never go out after work. I've two buses to get and they take even longer to come at night, so it's near twelve when I get back and I don't want to be out any later. And I can't afford a taxi cos it'll be about a tenner.

And anyway. I've got a three litre bottle of White Lightning I sneaked in yesterday after work. I hid it in my wardrobe, beside the kettle and wrapped up in a hoodie.

Niall goes red again. When he pulls the shutter down he says, —Do you want to head on now, Lisa, get your bus?

I'm like a rat up a drainpipe, getting out. And back at the hostel I have my White Lightning, all on my own and it's fucking lovely.

13.

The next thing with the gulag was, me and Chrissie fell out.

It was at school it happened. After me and Rocky shagged it was worse about Chrissie somehow. Maybe cos I'd something else to think about. Maybe cos I didn't like Chrissie in school, she sort of took the piss and made sly digs and then said she was only joking. I was right maybe that she only let on to like me cos we were in the gulag together. She didn't like me getting on better with Rocky either I don't think, she wanted all the attention.

I was thinking about Rocky the next morning, the morning after we shagged. I'd never been into a fella before. I'd have thought I was gay except I knew I wasn't. But Rocky was maybe different, maybe cos he was older. He didn't ignore me cos I didn't look like a supermodel, and I didn't think he'd tell people we'd shagged so I'd be called a SLUT in the street.

And it was proper shagging, adult stuff. It was a bit sore but maybe it wouldn't be after a bit, and anyway being a bit sore at first was probably cos of being with someone older?

There's worse sex to have.

Anyway, me and Chrissie were in the corridor after form class when I was thinking all this, we were going to English. We were in different classes for that cos I was put down for GCSE and Chrissie wasn't (not that I'd be doing any exams, I'd be well away by then), but our classrooms were beside each other.

—What're you daydreaming about? Chrissie said. Blared, the way she did.

She hit me in the arm with her schoolbag. I was hungover and she nearly scared the shit out of me.

—Nothing, I said. But it wouldn't have convinced a deaf six year old.

She looked, hard, leering. My face went hot, just to give me away.

—I bet you're thinking about Rocky—

I looked round to see who could hear here. Loads of people—

—You looooooove him—

—No I don't, right—

—Yeah you do, you looooove him, you love Rocky—

She was really loud. She always sounded like a foghorn, specially when trying to scunder someone. Someone behind us said,—Rocky? Like in them boxing films?

Chrissie let on to near choke at that, she was like a cat coughing up a furball.

It was Tracy and Suzanne from our form class behind us, and behind them most of the class.

Chrissie had an audience now so she puffed up.

—No, she said, —he's this fella she's shagging at the Rossway flats, but he doesn't look like Rocky, he looks like Freddie Mercury. Isn't that right Lisa, didn't you say to me the first night we went round that he looks like Freddie Mercury—

I had roaring in my head, proper roaring like holding a shell to my ear. She'd said I was shagging him, she'd said it in front of everyone and now they were listening and they'd say I was a slut—

A couple of people laughed.

I shouted,

—No I'm not, Chrissie, all right!

—You're not what, she said, —not saying he looks like Freddie Mercury or not shagging him?

I shouted again.

—I'm not shagging him!

People crowded around, pulled in by the noise and hoping for a fight. Chrissie laughed. Hard, she might as well have had her hands on her knees and her head threw back. If she wasn't such a fat mamma bitch, and yeah that's what she was a fat bitch and I didn't care if I didn't like people saying that cos I was fat too – anyway, if Chrissie wasn't such a fat mamma BITCH and would've killed me bouncing on top of me, I'd have fucking gone for her. I would.

Someone did the EastEnders music, the end bit. Someone else did Eye of the Tiger. People were in fits.

—Doof doof DOOF—

—Who's she meant to have shagged? Rocky? What year's he in?

—Who is she anyway, is she that new one who's in that home?

I tried to see who said what. I must've looked wild I thought later, like trapped in the jungle among natives with spears sort of wild. Everyone smirked and sniggered, but not right in my face and loud, in a way I could jump on them for.

Chrissie still had that look, her hard smiley look. She waited. If I went mental sure of course it wasn't her fault—

I said,

—Well, you shagged his mate!

But it was too late. Chrissie laughed again and she blew me a kiss and went off down the corridor.

I was going to kill her. Really really kill her.

She was already at the door leading out to the car park after school, where we waited for the gulag staff to pick us up.

She ignored me, gazing away and humming a bit. I didn't want to talk to her either, but then Joanne or whoever was picking us up would notice and Try to Intervene.

Sure enough, Joanne took one look at us and put on her concerned face.

—What's up?

—Nothing, Chrissie said, swinging her bag into the minibus and climbing in after it, —Lisa's having a huff, that's all—

I was going to kill her.

14.

It's halfway through December.

Everyone's pissed it feels like, work parties all over the place and people in Santa hats crashing into the shop for smokes and wine. There's singing in the streets. Everyone's pissed and happy.

So when Niall says about a drink again I think fuck it. Drink's class cos it stops the buzzing in my head, and I haven't been out in months. I can scrounge drinks off Niall, I know he'll buy me them. So I say yeah.

We go to a pub five minutes from the shop. It's packed, heaving, with people around my age or only a bit older. They're not like me or any of the ones from the hostel. The girls all have shiny hair and loads of makeup and eyelashes near as far out as their noses.

Their clothes are different too, mostly jeans and T-shirts and trainers but I can see even in the dim that they're posh. Some of the girls have tiny skirts on, not like Chrissie's I set on fire, but swishy ones and leather jackets.

Their drinks are different as well, they've got glasses of wine or else wee bottles of beer with names I don't know.

I don't give a shit about how I look, not since fourteen. As long as I'm clean and my hair washed that'll do, and a lot of the time I don't even care about that. But I feel like a dick now, stupid and scruffy in my hoodie and trackie bottoms. Like someone's kid sister allowed to tag along.

I press against the wall and watch these people while Niall's getting the drinks. I'm trying to figure out why they're different, cos it's not just the clothes and the hair and the makeup. Maybe I'll be like them if I get a flat over here, I can come to pubs like this in nice jeans and T-shirts (I'm never wearing a short skirt). I can be different.

I'm not convincing even myself even as I write this down. I'll never be different.

Anyway. So Niall comes over with the drinks and then we just stand there, not talking cos the music's too loud. I feel like a dick so much my scalp's prickling with it.

Niall knows it. He shouts in my ear.

—Do you want to play pool?

It's something to do, so I shout back all right.

We go upstairs to the pool hall. He's shit at pool, same as me, so two games takes ages. And I can feel myself getting pissed now cos the roaring's muffled in my head and I'm thinking fuck it, about everything. He buys shots, Jägermeister and sambuca and a Jägerbomb. I keep missing the white ball but I don't care. It's a laugh, I'm having a laugh. It's been fucking ages.

We go out to the beer garden and the lights are doing double. I don't have to think about anything apart from now, the bar, tonight.

—I've no fucking clue how I'm going to get home! I shout at Niall over the music. I play it up a bit, all laughy and helpless, cos maybe then he'll pay my taxi. He knows I'm on the dole. He knows I'm skint.

He shouts back,

—Stay at mine, sure!

People beside us hear him. There's a wolf whistle. There's laughing.

Niall sees my face.

—Just to save you a taxi! he shouts. —I'll sleep on the couch!

Like I've never heard that before.

It's like a balloon going down fast, how the night is gone now. Like water running down a plug, like music being snapped off. I nearly hear it, the night ending.

And I'm raging.

—Fuck off! I scream.

I push past the laughing guys around us and shove my way down the stairs and outside I'm fuming, raging. He's the same as them all, and I nearly fell for it again—

I've only one smoke left but I light it anyway.

I'm pissed and the buses stopped ages ago and I've no money. I'll have to walk home. It's about five miles but I'll have to.

I smoke. I psych myself up.

Niall's there. He looks like he's about to cry.

I wait. This is new. I've always had to back down with fellas, since ten and twelve and especially fourteen.

I wait.

—I didn't mean it like that, he says. I'm really sorry—

This is new too. I could get used to this. I suck hard and cross on my smoke, and I listen, not looking at him.

—I didn't mean to insult you, he says.

He meant what he said upstairs, he says, I can crash in his bed and he'll take the floor. Only so I don't have to bother getting home, I can get a bus in the morning—

So I go back to his flat. Well, he says he has drink.

It's a bedsit, where he lives. It's brilliant.

It's not much bigger than my hostel room but there's a kitchen. Just a tiny one, a kitchenette they're called, but there's a proper cooker and an oven and loads of cupboards. The whole bedsit is clean and new too, I can still smell the paint. There's proper furniture, even a squishy armchair. It's far nicer than the hostel. It's brilliant, I know it before I'm even in through the door.

I ask Niall if the bedsit's Housing Executive but he says it's private rental. Fuck, I think, cos I can't afford private rental, but then I ask him how much the rent is and he says it's two hundred quid a month. I think fast, more fast than normal cos my head's whirling with sambuca.

I can get most of that on Housing Benefit. They won't pay for a flat cos that's too dear, but this is the same cost as a room in a shared house, and Gemma said to me ages ago they'll pay for that OK, I just needed to get the money for the deposit and the first month's rent.

But if I get a place like this I'll have it all on my own.

And then I'll get a job, cash in hand, come off the dole and no-one'll know where I am.

I'm buzzing now, I'm nearly bouncing around the flat cos this is a way out. I thought I'd have to be loaded to get my own place, that it'd never happen. I knew it'd make me sick to share a flat again, but I thought I'd no choice. I didn't know about bedsits.

The deposit's two hundred a month as well, Niall says. Four hundred quid's loads more money than I've ever seen, but I don't care. Two hundred quid deposit and two hundred first month's rent.

I'm going to do it.

I can hardly sit still on Niall's bed. I'll get the four hundred quid. I'm twenty at in the middle of April, I'm going to do it for then. I'll go out to the pub as well, raise a glass to the end of my teens.

I'll get the four hundred quid. I don't know how but I'll get it.

. . .

15.

By the Thursday after me and Chrissie fell out I was going mental, I was about to punch someone.

I was just getting through to the next night so I could go round to Rocky's like he'd said. Maybe he had a nice flat with Sky and we could curl on the couch all evening. I'd probably have to shag him at least once, but we could lie under a blanket and smoke blow and watch TV—

Thursday night I just went to my room and said I was doing homework when Joanne knocked on the door. —Do you want to talk about it? she said and I said no. —Do you want me to get Chrissie here so you can both Talk It Through? she said, and I said NO.

—It might be better to get it all out in the open, she said, like a dog with a bone, so then I said it, I told her to fuck off.

Her eyes went all wide and she got two spots of colour on her cheeks, right away like someone had pinched her. There was a big long pause while the *fuck off* echoed about. Then she said,

—I don't think that's the most constructive language to use, do you, Lisa?

And I lost it, I got up off the bed and I shouted at her, —I SAID fuck off, will you FUCK OFF—

I went to move towards the door, like a dog baring its teeth, and she closed it quick and then I could hear her footsteps going away and down the corridor. Fuck her.

It was my birthday that day, I was fifteen.

And then, finally, it was Friday and school was over and I'd been given my pocket money for the week and I was going to see Rocky.

I had a shower and then put on my jeans and my black jumper again, and I tried to put on some of the makeup Mandy had bought me as well but it looked stupid without Chrissie doing it for me so I took it off.

Chrissie was coming up the stairs when I left my room. She looked at me as I passed, her face like licking a toilet bowl someone just pissed on. She was daring me to say something, I could feel it. And I shouldn't have, cos she could've made it really shit for me in the gulag and in school, but I was going to Rocky's now so I didn't need her or any of them. So I said at her, —What the fuck are you looking at—

—You, you ugly bitch—

And then I couldn't say anything else, cos that was true and if I tried to take her up on it I knew I'd cry.

Rocky waited for me at the block's front door.

—You're late, he said.

I said,—Sorry, cos if he was pissed off I'd have to go back to the gulag. But he laughed and said he was only messing.

—Come on, he said, and we went to the lift.

His flat was way up at the top of the block. The lift was rickety and I was freaked in case it broke, I couldn't stand being closed in somewhere even then.

The corridor we got out on had boarded up doors and spray paint on the walls and wire mesh on the windows. The council was going to fix it, he said. Only him and another fella lived on this floor even though there were ten flats.

—I like it, Rocky said. —You get a bit of peace—

His flat had a wooden door, the sort the council put on when they kick someone out, a thick heavy one covered in bolts. It was cos he'd only moved in a couple of weeks ago he said and they hadn't fixed it yet.

He shoved the door open and we went in.

It was dark, and it smelt a bit, like the squat in Belfast. I was nervous now, but I thought I was being a kid.

But there were voices in the living room.

My stomach clenched. I thought it'd be just us, I didn't want to be in a flat with a load of people, fellas, I didn't know. Chrissie talked enough for both of us, but I couldn't do it on my own. I didn't like meeting new people, especially fellas. I still don't.

But it was OK. There were two fellas, but Rocky said, —Right lads, time to fuck off—

And they grinned and went out, no bother.

—They hang around here sometimes when I'm out, Rocky said, —but it's my flat really.

I looked round. There was no cosy couch or big telly and Sky box. Just a raggedy ripped couch and a beanbag on the floor. There was a telly, but a tiny portable on a chair with a video player on top. A stereo on the floor, and a wooden crate with a cup and plate on it. The plate had dried bean juice on it. I hoped Rocky hadn't been spending all his money on drink for me—

I sat, kind of perched on the edge of the couch. I felt nervous. Writing it now's making me think of Niall the night we shagged, the way the air sort of crackled with what we both knew would happen.

Rocky took my shoulders and pushed me back.

—Chill, he said. —What's wrong with you?

I sat up. I didn't know what was wrong. He'd been nice to me, lovely, and I was sitting like I had a poker up my arse.

He sat beside me.

—You all right? he said and I nodded yeah.

—Get some of this into you, he said.

It was a bottle of vodka.

I drank.

We did do it, I knew we would. But later, lying under the blanket, I got telling him about Chrissie and how everyone at school knew me and Rocky were shagging.

—Are you scundered about me, is that it? he said.

—No!

—I'm only messing, he said. —Don't worry about her. She's a stupid cunt, I don't know what Jim sees in her—

My heart lifted. You never know someone's reaction when you say another person's pissed you off, the person you're telling might think you're paranoid or a dick. Or sort of agree but think you're overreacting. But when they get it, when someone Gets It and agrees 100%, well, it's the best feeling ever.

I snuggled into him. The shagging had been nearly not sore this time. I said, fishing,

—Is she?

I was dying to slag Chrissie off. I had for ages but I couldn't to Petesy and Darren or anyone at school in case they told her.

—She is, he said, —she's too loud and she talks too much. And she needs to lay off the pies, have you seen the size of her—

I went quiet. Chrissie was fatter than me but that didn't make me skinny.

He copped on.

—But you, he said, —you're gorgeous—

—No I'm not, I said.

I was pissed off. He was only saying it, like patting me on the head.

—You are, he said.

I couldn't say no again, cos that'd be fishing. So I lay there. I felt like crying.

He reached under the blanket and grabbed my tit.

—You are, he said again, —and don't let anyone tell you different—

He said,

—I want you to be my girlfriend, would you be my girlfriend?

I ducked my head under the blanket and brought it back up again with my face red.

—Um, OK, I said, scundered.

But he laughed, in a nice way. He said I was cute. And I stopped thinking I was a dick and laughed with him too.

We did it again after that. It was sorer than before, I don't know why. I cried out, but he said *ssh, ssh*, and kissed me as he kept moving. He went on for ages and it hurt more. I moaned under him, trying to move away, but he must've thought me wriggling and moaning was me turned on, cos he went even harder.

I closed my eyes and waited for it to be over. I was still getting used to him. It wouldn't be as sore next time maybe.

After he finished he put his arm around my shoulder and I lay with my head on his chest. He put his hand down and stroked my pubes, playing with them and twisting them round his finger.

I tried to relax into it. It was warm under the blanket at least, and it wasn't so sore now he was out of me.

—We should maybe think about getting you a trim, he said into my shoulder.

I kind of knew what he meant but I wasn't sure.

—A what?

He pushed himself up on one shoulder.

—A trim, he said. —You know, down there. A wax, like. It'd be sexy—

—Is that not sore? I said.

He said it wasn't, not really, loads of girls had it done these days.

I didn't know about it. I'd heard of it, course I had, everyone had. But like, did loads of girls have it done? It sounded fucked up—

—It's really sexy, he said. —Like, really *really* sexy.

His voice had a kind of plea. I was a bitch. He was trying to ask without asking outright. I was his girlfriend now, and you were meant to do stuff for your boyfriend, I knew that even if I'd never been a girlfriend before.

—OK, I said, and he grabbed me and hugged me and told me I was class.

Rocky put a video on, to show me how sexy the others girls were with their waxings. He had one borrowed from a mate, he said, Raymie who'd been there earlier.

—Wait til you see this, he said.

He passed me the rest of the vodka. He rolled a spliff and fiddled with the video player.

—Wait til you see, he said.

The TV screen blurred. Then it was black and flickering, then flesh-coloured and blurry and a woman going *Oh oh oh*.

I couldn't figure it out. I could hear the woman but it was just dark and flesh-coloured patches on the screen. Then the camera pulled away and it was a very close closeup of a man and a woman shagging. She was wide open and he slammed into her nearly like he hated her, and she screamed the whole time *Oh oh oh*.

She was so... open. It was the first time I'd seen another woman. It looked like a gash. Maybe that's how it looks when you've done it loads? Maybe I was doing it wrong, not going *Oh oh oh* like that—

—See? Rocky said. —She's had a wax, look—

She was bald, and kind of shiny, like Lambert the science teacher under the light or leaning over the Bunsen burner. She looked waxed. Not her pubes, all of her, waxed and shiny like a new car.

—Yeah, I said.

But I couldn't concentrate on how she looked cos this huge thing slammed into her and all I could hear was her screeching. Was it pain screeching or sex screeching? I didn't know the difference. The guy looked like he hated her. His face twisted up and you could tell he was doing it to her as hard as he could. It was scary but I didn't know why.

We watched more. I stared at the screen and I sucked hard on the spliff. The woman kept going *Oh oh oh*, and the fella kept at her like he wanted to rip her open.

It looked sore, but I didn't want to say. So I said instead, —She's got loads of stamina doesn't she—

I laughed, cos of sounding lighthearted.

—Oh yeah, Rocky said, —she's great. She takes it and takes it, no bother, she's good.

He looked at me.

I'd tried not to let on earlier it was sore. I'd tried to take it no bother. But he must've noticed, was this why he'd put the porno on? He was older than me and he must've had lots of girls. They probably took it as good as the shiny woman did—

Chrissie was right, I was a baby. I hated her but I bet she took it like that. Took it better than me—

Another girl came in. The guy stopped with the first one, and he grabbed the second one by the hair and shoved her face downwards. The camera went down too. He shoved his dick in her mouth, right in. She looked delighted, like it tasted of strawberries and cream. The camera pulled back to show them both. The man looked like he hated her as well. He rammed into her face, I thought she'd choke.

—Go on, go on, Rocky said softly.

The guy pulled out and started wanking.

—Here, Rocky said, —wait til you see this—

And the fella grabbed the girl by the hair again and pushed her down and came all over her face.

—Mmmm, she went, still acting all delighted. —Mmmm—

It looked, I don't know, not sexy, but… something. It was proper shagging. Adult stuff.

It was scary but a bit exciting as well. Cos now I was thinking, could I take it like them girls? Could I?

But maybe I'd do wrong. I'd never given a blowjob, I'd maybe fuck it up and Rocky would know.

I looked at him, a sneaky glance like I wasn't.

And it was like we were right in tune, like totally right for each other and like the couple in the porno, cos right then Rocky looked at me too. I knew what he wanted even before he threw the blanket off and stood up and pulled me over.

He had me on the floor, kneeling, and my knees hurt and he pulled my hair and shoved into me. And it hurt and I choked but I couldn't stop cos he gripped my hair so tight. I didn't want to stop, I wanted to show him. And then there was something scalding and rancid in my throat, bitter and metallic like sucking on coins. I swallowed it fast, cos I was a bit scared, and the taste was even worse.

He let me go. My my neck was sore, cos my head had been twisted half round. I tried to get up but my knees buckled cos they were sore from kneeling, and my throat hurt as well.

And I thought, what the fuck's the point of that, it was sore and it tasted rancid, was I meant to get something out of it like the girl on the porno?

He pulled me up onto the couch with him.

—You're class, he said, —you can take it every bit as good as them girls—

The burning and the hurt didn't matter. I leaned my head on his chest. His heart thumped and banged against my ear. Maybe I'd do it again if he asks, I thought, cos I can take it. Cos it makes him happy and cos that's what girlfriends do.

16.

I wanted to stay over, have a night together. But he said to go back to the gulag so I didn't get into shit.

—You know what them social workers are like, he said, —and I don't want them trying to stop you seeing me—

—I don't care, I said. —I want to stay here—

—And I'd love you to stay, sweetheart, he said. —But we'll keep them sweet for now, and sort you staying later on, all right?

I could stay over another time. And no-one had ever called me *sweetheart*, and it gave me warm fuzzies. So I got dressed, shivering in the chill after the blanket.

—Good girl, he said, and that gave me warm fuzzies too.

He said he'd walk me home. I was chuffed, cos now I'd have him a bit longer before going back into my life.

When we left he put his arm around me, cos I was so cold my teeth chattered. —It's all right, baby, he said, —we'll have you home in no time—

I cuddled into him the whole way home. He cared about me, he didn't want me getting into trouble, and he cared that I was cold.

He left me at the end of the drive. He kissed me, deep. He asked if I wanted to come round tomorrow, in the daytime. My heart went warm and I said yeah.

—Cool, he said. —Come round whenever. I'll be in.

And he kissed me on the forehead. And he was gone.

I staggered up the drive, trying not to make noise on the gravel. I wanted to hug myself. I always thought that was a dicky expression, but I knew what it meant. I could've wrapped my arms around me and given me a big hug. I'd try it upstairs, in my room—

The front door opened. It was Sean, looking tragic.

—Thank you for coming home on time, Lisa, he said as I lurched past him, cos that's what social workers do when the Young People do something they're meant.

So I said, all grand,

—You're welcome. Sean.

He tried not to show it, but he had the hump. He followed me into the hall.

—Have you been drinking? he said.

—No, I said, even though it must've been totally obvious, cos my eyes felt tiny and I must've stunk of vodka and blow.

A big giggle bubbled in my chest like it hadn't for ages. I said,

—I assure you, Sean, that I haven't touched a single drop—

I can still see his face, after I said it and I was heading up the stairs. I could see him knowing I was blocked, but maybe he should leave it cos I was home in time and cos I was going upstairs cheerful and co-operative. None of the staff had seen me cheerful.

So I trilled at him, —Goodnight Sean!

And I got up the stairs and into my room and fell on the bed laughing so hard into my pillow I was nearly sick.

And I hugged myself. Life was brilliant.

I still felt class the next morning. (He'd called me sweetheart and baby). I even said hi to Chrissie at breakfast, and laughed at her stupid round FAT face going *does not compute*. I laughed at her and I left to see my boyfriend.

17.

We don't shag, me and Niall, the night we play pool. I conk out on his bed instead. I'm pissed, shitfaced, but I make sure to starfish anyway, in case he tries to climb up beside me. I know that move.

It's grey in the room when I wake, there's dawn at the curtains. Niall's on the floor, curled up like a kid. So I get my shoes and coat on and I sneak out. I don't want to talk – I never do in the mornings, before I get my mind straight to face people – and anyway my head's banging like a fucking builder's at it.

I check myself. My tracksuit bottoms are still all the way up and my knickers are still on. I don't have that raw feeling and my knickers don't feel damp. So probably Niall didn't shag me when I was asleep—

Maybe he thought about it. But he didn't do it so maybe he's all right. I'll keep my guard up though. Just in case.

But. The next time, I let him do it.

We're out at the pub again cos I think fuck it again and then when we get back to the bedsit I think fuck it about that as well. Niall likes me and he wants to shag me and we're pissed and I can't be arsed making it a big deal or having to do a talk. Like how do you say that anyway. No I don't want to have sex with you, put your dick back where it's meant. *Like seriously, how do you say it. And what the fuck then? I'd have to have left, cos we'd both be too scundered to look at each other, and then I'd be out in the ballfreezing cold having to walk five miles home.*

How the shag finally happens is, I go back to the bedsit with Niall cos he has beer. We have to sit on the bed cos there's no couch, and I know he's thinking of making a move. He doesn't know I know but I do. He sits a bit too close, the way fellas do before lunging. He asks about the hostel and I say it's all right.

It's fucking stupid, this, it's shite, we both know it's talk before his move.

I never said I was In Care, before, I don't want him to know. Not like, no-one must never know! *but cos so fucking what. But I tell him anyway, now, on his bed. Probably I'm trying to put him off.*

I sound like Chrissie when I tell him, and I remember that night, that first night in the flat with More-the-Merrier and Freddie Mercury and me and her, us listening as she spilled her guts.

I leave stuff out. I only tell him about before the gulag, about my ma and Paul and why I was put In Care. I leave a lot of stuff out. I don't say about Rocky.

Niall's on the level, maybe. I can't tell cos course I've thought that before, when I was a stupid cunt. But he's like a kid listening to a story, listening hard, nearly crying when I say about Paul beating me up. (He doesn't know the half of it. I could have him in floods. Beating his chest and wailing to the heavens like women you see at funerals on the news.)

I nearly laugh but I don't. It's not Niall's fault he's like this, it's cos of where he's from and cos he's a student and he grew up different. He's all right. It's not his fault he's the sort of fella who'd probably get a kicking and his wallet emptied within a day in the hostel—

Maybe he thinks I'll cry. So he can brush my tears away with his thumb, and cup my chin in his hand, and lean in for a soft, soft kiss. But when I finish, he's looking at his trainers.

—I don't know what to say that's so awful I'm so sorry, he says.

The silence stretches. I don't know what to say either. And I know he's still thinking about the move.

Songs slam in my head sometimes. Or phrases, banging around inside me like chants. They started when I was fourteen. Three is a magic number *is one of them. The word* wankbank, *fast over and over.*

Here, as I pull Niall down on the bed and make the move myself cos can't he get it over with, the song pounding in my head is I'm just a girl who can't say no.

After, he smiles at me. Like this shag is the best thing that's happened to him in all his puff.

I smile back at him, pretending.

18.

Rocky opened the door and grinned.

—C'mere, you—

When we got up to his flat he kissed me. He did it hard, almost like a porno, but I kissed him back.

He pulled away. He looked into my face. He did it intense and I giggled but he said *ssh*.

He pushed his tracksuit bottoms down. He wanted a shag I thought, but he looked more into my face and he put his hands on my shoulders and pushed me to the floor. He thrust himself in my face and I caught on.

It choked me again, but I did it. Cos I could.

—Will we go into town? he said after.

He pulled me up. I wiped my mouth with my hand when he wasn't looking.

I was hyper about going into town with him. He didn't mind being seen with me, he wanted us to go out together.

He put his arm around me, and I swelled up chuffed. If Chrissie could see me now, or even Sean or Joanne, they'd see how I didn't need them—

A whistle and a shout nearly deafened me.

—YEOOOOW ROCKY!

Someone ran over to us. But Rocky kept his arm around my shoulder anyway.

—All right, Raymie?

It was a fella from the flat the night before. He looked me up and down the way fellas do. But it wasn't like the normal way, like thinking straight off fuck no. He looked… interested. Had Rocky said I was his girlfriend?

They talked about a car Raymie saw and if Rocky could get a hundred quid they could have the car between them by that night. —No can do, Rocky said. Then he said, —You know Lisa, right?

Raymie looked at me again. —Nice to meet you, Lisa, he said, and I mumbled, —Nicetomeetyoutoo. Chrissie would've had fits laughing.

But he nodded and smiled (he had brown teeth) and he said to Rocky, —Well sure let me know about the car, and he was away, loping across the square towards the flats.

Rocky's phone beeped with a text. He laughed when he read it.

—Look, he said.

It was from Raymie. *Lisa hot!!* it said. *Lt me no if u dont want her no more lol!!*

—Yeah right, I said.

Raymie was just saying it, being nice to Rocky. But Rocky said no, Raymie texted last night and said who's the girl came into the flat.

—I reckon he fancies you, Rocky said.

—Yeah right, I said again. But I smiled anyway. Raymie had brown teeth but still. Maybe I wasn't that fat and ugly after all.

Town was packed, it was like the whole of Craigavon had woke up and thought c'mon go shopping in Lurgan. Maybe my ma and Paul would be here. It'd be like the shopping centre, only now Rocky was here to look after me.

We might see them in a shop. Rocky's arm would be around my shoulder again. And Paul would say something to my ma, something bad about me. Rocky would hear them, he'd storm up to Paul like, *what did you say about my girlfriend!* He'd shout, *you'd better say sorry to her*! Paul would say *no chance*, and Rocky would deck him.

And Paul would stagger back into a rail of clothes, that would land on him like a scene in a film.

It sounds stupid now. But I was stupid.

Rocky interrupted my daydream.

—C'mon in here a minute—

We went into an 02 shop and Rocky went over to an assistant. He's getting a topup for his phone I thought, so I loitered and looked at the phones and wished I'd loads of money.

But Rocky called me over. And he said,

—Here. This is for you.

And it was a phone. A new, shiny, red, new, phone. For me.

It was a proper phone. Not a massive one at £9.99 without even texting on it, and that would've been fine anyway. This was tiny, fitting snug in my palm, and the screen flipped up. —You can text with it, Rocky said, —you can be in touch with me any time you want—

It was gorgeous. It was the gorgeous thing I've had in my life, even now. It was so gorgeous and it was mine.

But. It was £79.99. And Rocky asked for £20 of topup. I tugged at his sleeve. I tried to tell him.

—It's too dear, I hissed.

—Ach, ssh, Rocky said. He and the sales fella laughed. Rocky said,

—The money doesn't matter. You need a phone, so have a proper one—

A bubble of happiness came up in my chest like the night before.

—Can you afford it? I said.

The sales fella laughed.

—You don't hear that often from girls in this shop, he said. Rocky looked at me and smiled, all soft.

—This one's different, he said.

I was happy happy happy.

We went to Cafolla's for lunch, we a plate of chips and an ice cream float each. Rocky wouldn't let me pay. We sat at a tiny table with my new phone and Rocky laughed at me, cos I couldn't take my eyes off it.

The shop fella had charged it a bit, so Rocky showed me how to work it. He showed me the text part and the contacts part.

—Here's your most important number, he said. He saved ROCKY into Contacts and told me to send him a text.

It was my first ever text, how sad is that? So I fumbled with it and he had to saying things like *that button there*, and *hit select*, and everyone in Cafolla's would think I was special needs. But I pressed Send, and right away there was the beepbeep of his phone.

—Now I'll save your number, he said, and he typed something fast and showed me.

SWEETHEART, it said, right above my number.

—Ach, I said, going red. But it was that exact moment, in Cafolla's in Lurgan with our sandwich wrappers and drink cups on the table between us, that I knew I loved him.

And I was happy happy happy.

We walked around town. He kept his arm around me and maybe we'd see Chrissie or my ma and Paul—

—Seen enough? Rocky said.

He glared behind him.

—What? I said.

He said,

—That old bat who passed us, she gave me a dirty look cos I'd my arm round you.

—What for? I said.

—Fuck knows, she maybe thinks I'm too old for you, or no-one should have their arm round someone—

He spat on the ground.

—Fuck her, he said, —fucking old bat—

It was the first time I'd ever seen him pissed off. I wanted to hide a bit, cos people were looking. But he was right. Fuck her, fuck the old bat, fuck all of them.

19.

Rocky stopped outside a shop.

—Do you want to? he said. —For me?

It was a beauty parlour. I'd never stepped a toe into a place like that, they weren't for fat girls.

But I knew what he meant. He wanted me to have the waxing. Get tidied up and look like women in pornos and not like a reject from the 70s. Everyone did it these days. He'd said. But I didn't think he'd meant right away. What if I was smelly – down there?

—Please? he said. I heard myself saying all right. I'd said the night before that I would. And anyway there was the phone. This was a little thing he wanted. I couldn't say no.

He took me inside the shop.

It was bright and shiny, all lights and mirrors and chrome and perfume. The staff were glam and fake tanned with styled hair and orange makeup. I used to, still do, hate being around girls like that, cos it's like they look down their noses at me, cos I don't know about makeup properly and cos my hair's like rats' tails. I used to think girls like that were millies with their two hours to get ready in the morning, but I also thought if I could look like that I'd take two hours to get ready too.

I don't care now. I suppose I'd like to look nice, but it's easier not being noticed.

A woman came over, all smiles and can I help you. Claire, a badge on her white coat said. She glanced me up and down and decided – I could feel her, deciding – that it was Rocky who knew what to say.

I hung back. Was this woman, this stranger made up and perfect looking, going to see my bits?

—Full wax, Rocky said. She asked if it was my first time and he said yeah.

They mumbled a bit more and laughed.

Finally she turned to me.

—Will we go on through?

I looked at Rocky. I wanted him to say I obviously was too nervous, so I didn't have to.

—I'll see you out here after, he said.

So I followed her.

I followed her into a room that looked like a doctor's, with a surgical couch covered with paper towel. The light was even brighter here and soft music played from a tiny CD player on the windowsill.

I was sweating, all over. Like, all over.

—If you'd like to slip your jeans and knickers off and pop yourself up on the couch! she cooed at me.

I clambered up fast so she couldn't see my big white arse. I lay back, my fanny flashed up to the ceiling and the fear coming off me in waves I could smell.

—Push your knees up, that's it—

She was looking at my fanny! I'd never been as scundered, not then, not even when Chrissie said to the school I was shagging Rocky. Not even when Kelly at my old school made me cry. No-one had seen me there since my granny changed my nappy. Rocky, fellas, didn't count, cos when I had my bits out it was for shagging, and anyway fellas don't look like this woman did, intense like she should have had a miner's hat on—

My knees clenched together. She pushed them apart.

She wiped around me with something wet. My face burned. I stared at the ceiling, pretending I wasn't there. She painted around me with something hot.

—That's it now, she said, —you'll just feel a slight pull—

She was a lying cunt, cos there was a huge rip and a burn and I didn't even know I'd screamed until I stopped.

I scrambled myself up on my elbows.

I saw her with a yucky piece of paper she'd taken off me. The wax on it was brown and there was like a whole rug of pubes on there. I wanted to get off the table but my legs were too shaky to move.

My eyes were watering and soon I was crying for real.

—First one's always a bit nippy! she smiled at me, like all she'd done was take one hair out with tweezers and tickled me with a feather. Then she said, and at first I didn't think I'd heard her right, —A few more of those and we're done—

She pushed me back down again and all I thought for the next ages of minutes was *don't scream don't scream*. It was fucking agony, brutal, nothing had ever hurt as much, not even the first time with Rocky, it was fucking agony.

She did the ripping thing three more times, one big and two small but all as sore, and when I thought it was over at last she made me get up on my hands and knees and she did it again, then when I was lying down again she got a pair of tweezers and started on what she called the strays. That was even worse, every pluck she did my eyes watered again and after three or four they were streaming.

It went on for ever. Then — *thank fuck thank fuck* — the waxing woman smoothed something cool on me. Then, thank fuck thank fuck, she stepped away.

—There you go, she kind of sang, —all done!

I stumbled off the table. I found my knickers and jeans. I saw myself moving in front of me and it was a mirror, so I looked before I put my knickers on.

It was horrible. It was pink and raw looking and even with me being fat I looked like a little girl.

. . .

20.

But Rocky was really proud of me. He told me all the way home and then we were hardly in the door before he said he wanted a look, so to take my jeans and knickers off. I was scundered again. He'd never looked at me like that, up close and inspecty. I felt like a slab of cow in the market.

He looked up. He grinned.

—It's class, he said. —It's class. You're a brave girl. Come here—

And he pulled me onto the couch.

21.

I'm just back from work when Gemma calls me into the office. Maybe the staff's found my kettle or the new bottle of White Lightning I think, but she says there's a letter from the Housing Executive.

My head goes all swimmy and so does my stomach, cos it might be an offer, it might be a flat. Words jump out at me when I try and read the letter, it's like being wasted. Then I make the words out and I'm nearly crying then I'm nearly kicking the door. They're cunts, they're all cunts—

So the letter says cos I turned down the second flat they offered me, I've only got one more offer then they're Under No Obligation to house me after that. More than a year and a half I've been on the housing list and they want to boot me off it. You only get three goes and then they decide you're a fussy fucker and take you off the list.

I want to cry more cos they're totally wrong. I'm the fucking opposite of fussy. I'm a housing slag, I'd sleep in a garage in a sleeping bag if they let me. But the two flats I got offered – I just couldn't take them.

Here's what happened. The first offer I got was about six months ago, saying there was a flat in Lisburn and the viewing was on this date and let them know if I couldn't attend. If I couldn't attend, yeah right, I couldn't wait.

The viewing was in three days' time and I couldn't even sleep for thinking about it. I knew it wouldn't be a mansion, or even a normal size flat, but it'd be mine and there'd be my own door and a key.

But there were holes in the walls. Actual holes, huge, the size of car tyres. I could see the street through some of them. Parts of the floor were missing, so I went from door to wall on the foundations, like they were stepping stones in a piranha pool. The Housing Executive woman stayed at the door, cos she hoped I was a mug.

I thought maybe I'd take it anyway, even though I'd no money to do it up, even with a grant. There were no holes in the bedroom so maybe I could sleep in there. But I knew even if I was desperate I couldn't, it was dark and stinking and it'd make my head sicker.

I didn't cry back at the hostel but Gemma knew anyway. She rang them and said it wasn't not a reasonable offer cos the flat wasn't in a liveable state, *so they should remove it from the file. They said no, cos there was running water and the internal door worked and so did the smoke alarm, and that made it liveable beause it had all the relevant criteria.*

And I couldn't appeal, cos they're the ones who decide the relevant criteria.

So I thought, well I'll definitely take the next one. As long as it's got a floor.

The second offer was a couple of weeks ago. It was in Belfast this time, up near a loyalist estate. That flat was a dump as well and the streets a round it were smothered in Union Jacks and UDA flags. But I thought fuck it, I'd risk it.

But then there was the wallpaper.

The Housing Executive fella showed me the living room and it was all right even if it did smell. Then he showed me the bedroom, and there was grubby white wallpaper with twisted yellow and pink flowers, like there'd been in the B&B, and next thing I knew I was out on the street and running away. So now this letter says I didn't complete the viewing, so it counts as a rejected offer so I only have one left.

Maybe the last one will be OK (yeah right, I think, but maybe it will). There's a new build opening soon, maybe next year, not in the university bit of Belfast but down at the old docks. That's one of my areas of choice, cos the docks are a total dump and hardly anyone lives there, and if you pick a shit area there's more chance getting a place. But there's only three one-bedroom flats in the new build, and maybe I've gone down the list anyway cos of turning these two flats down. Even if I couldn't take them. Even if one had holes in the walls and the floor, and the other made me remember. PTSD, that's called, I saw it on telly. It shouldn't count.

Gemma says the hostel staff will help when I find somewhere. They'll help me paint or plaster, she says, so I know she thinks the next flat, my last offer, will be shit too.

—Would you not reconsider the second one? Gemma says. —If they haven't offered it to someone else?

I can't tell her why not. So I say something you're allowed to in Belfast.

—It's the estate, I say. —I wouldn't feel comfortable, with the flags and murals—

It's their language I use as well, so she nods. You can say that here, that you can't live somewhere cos it's a Different Community. And it's not being snobby or sectarian either, cos everyone knows you get checked out when you move somewhere like that and you get petrolbombed out if you're not right. Like Gemma's friend, a fella from the south who moved into a loyalist estate, a petrol bomb smashed through his window within a week.

She tells me I'll have to take the third offer, no matter where it is, but if I'm really really uncomfortable with it she'll try and appeal.

—It's not fair, she says.

I think she means it, but I can't talk about it anymore. I reach for the door handle.

—There's sandwiches in the kitchen, Gemma says. —A couple of donations came in—

This is the best time of year in the hostel, cos people get Christmassy and drop stuff off to the poor homeless. It's normally big trays of sandwiches left over from office parties, but sometimes there's cakes or tins of biscuits as well. Most days around this time in December I don't even have to buy any food or go into my box in my room. The staff love it too, I don't think they get paid much.

I'm starving so I make up a plate to take upstairs, of triangled sandwiches and cocktail sausages and those pastry things called vole something. I'm piling the plate high when Debbie comes in.

Debbie's been here about a month. She's all right. She knows Chrissie from a home they were in years ago, she says she thought Chrissie was a dick. (She asked me if I knew where Chrissie is now, cos she's not in any of the hostels, but I haven't seen her since the fire.)

Debbie's skinny with dyed black hair and white skin and spots and she's got scars all sliced up and down her arms like me. There's rumours about her, I hear stuff. Her phone beeps then a car's outside for her, and she's away for about an hour then she's always got money when she comes back. She doesn't hide it, she comes into the lounge and gives people money and smokes she owes them and she maybe orders a Chinese.

We know what she's doing, but I'm probably the only one who knows properly.

She gets hassled. We're the only girls in here, there's sixteen fellas and they crawl over her, like flies. (They used to do it to me but they stopped after a few months.) They stand too close and say stuff about blowjobs, saying it like joking in case the staff hear. Nothing ever happens about it, even if the staff do hear.

I wonder about Debbie. About her Before. She knew a Blackheads, I think. Maybe she knew a Rocky.

Maybe I'll ask her. Say something all casual and simple, like Need any help with your mate who rings? That's how I can make money for my deposit and first month's rent, I could be in a bedsit like Niall's in no time. Twenty quid a time would make it – I work it out – thirty times. Thirty stinking fat oul fellas probably, but I've had far worse and far more than that.

It'd take me two weeks if it was two fellas a day. I can do two a day easy, that's wee buns. And if it's more than twenty quid each time then that's even faster.

Debbie feels my look. She puts on a face.

NO, my head goes. NO.

So I look away.

And I've just got it, up here in my room, it's like one of those cartoons with a lightbulb over someone's head. I work in a shop, for fuck's sake. A shop with a till, and loads of money, I must touch hundreds of quid just in a week.

I'll have to be careful, course I will. But I think I can nick it from the Spar.

TWO

Room

1.

After the waxing, after we shagged, Rocky said I should go back to the gulag. Raymie was coming over, it was arranged for ages and Rocky couldn't get out of it.

—Can't be helped, sweetheart, Rocky said. —I'd rather be with you, you know I would—

It was stupid, pathetic, that I felt shit about it. Like he'd got rid of me. He'd bought me a phone and I was an ungrateful bitch. Maybe I'd text him tomorrow, say *hows it goin*. Maybe he'd text back *sure why not call round*.

It was nearly tea time when I got back to the gulag. I sneakied a look through the glass in the door of the living room to see if Chrissie was there, but it was safe. Petesy was there but I ignored him, he'd be on Chrissie's side cos they'd shagged—

So I took my phone out. Maybe to play with it but maybe to show off as well. Petesy saw right away.

—Is that a new phone, lemme see—

The door banged open.

—Food's ready! Chrissie shouted, all up her own arse about it like she'd cooked the dinner and dug up the spuds herself. So I put my phone in my pocket.

But Petesy opened his big trap over tea. Chrissie's phone binged with a text, and she made a big show out of reading it, smirking so we'd all know a fella had sent it. And Petesy said to her and Darren, in front of Tommy and the two staff as well,

—Here, have you seen Lisa's new phone?

My cheeks were scarlet, right away. Chrissie smirked more.

—Can I see? Steve the staff said.

I had to hand it over. He examined it, turning it over and flipping up the screen. I was ready to snatch it off him if he tried to read my text, but he didn't.

—Where did you get this, Lisa? he asked. All serious. —It must have cost a fair bit—

Everyone waited. Chrissie smirked.

—Someone bought me it, I said at last.

—Who?

They waited.

—A mate, I said.

Chrissie whooped, in her foghorn voice.

—I bet it was her boyfriend. Is that right, Lisa, was it your BOYFRIEND?

—Lisa mightn't want to share her confidential information with the entire dining room, Steve said, the two-faced ballbag.

But Chrissie cackled, and I went more red, so everyone knew she'd hit the tit on the nipple and a boyfriend had bought the phone.

I hated that place. I hated it hated it hated it, where everyone knew my business and dicks like Chrissie took the piss. I wanted to be at Rocky's. All the time.

It was Saturday so they were all going out, and Chrissie was tarting herself up in her room. So the living room was mine. I lay full down on the couch so no-one could sit beside me, just in case, and I put the telly on, You've Been Framed or some shite like that so I had charge of the remote and could say I Was Here First if anyone had a go.

The door banged again, Chrissie couldn't come through a door normally even if she was bribed with all of Boyzone bare and ribboned on a plate. I didn't move my legs. She sat in the armchair. I watched the telly. She looked at me, I could feel it. I flicked through the channels.

—Where'd you get the phone? she said at last, when it was say something or burst, Chrissie would talk to her own shite if there was no-one to listen. She was talking cos she was bored.

—Rocky, I said. I couldn't be arsed rowing. I wanted her to fuck off.

—Looks dear, she said, —was it dear?

—Yeah, I said.

There was a long, long pause. I read a book that said *pregnant pause* once, it was like that. She was nearly flipping, she wanted a fight or for me to spill the beans.

I'd have been a jellied wreck a week before, in case she had a go. But now — now I nearly laughed in her fat face.

She simmered. She boiled. She boiled over. She leaned nearly out of the armchair, her face all shiny and red.

—You needn't think you ARE someone cos someone's shagging you, Lisa O' Neill, she said, all fast. —Everyone at school and everyone in here thinks you're a stupid ugly bitch. And they won't STOP thinking you're a stupid ugly bitch just cos you opened your legs to some fella who looks like Freddie Mercury—

I didn't decide to. I didn't weigh it up like ho hum maybe that's a good idea or maybe it's not oh well I'll do it anyway. And I don't know why people witter violence isn't the answer, cos sometimes it is, sometimes people need a thump.

I threw the remote control at her, hard. It bounced off her head, ha.

Then I was up and at her.

I had her from the start cos she was sitting. I waded into her. I grabbed her ponytail and banged her head off the back of the chair. She kicked me but I couldn't feel it, I never did in those days. I held her hair in one hand and I got her big flabby cheek in the other, and I squeezed, digging my nails into her fat stupid face.

She screeched. I didn't care. She kicked out hard and I fell back, and we were on the floor and she crushed me. I'd be smothered to death—

But I got a hand free. And I reached up and I jabbed my finger into her eye. As hard as I could.

I'd never done that, not to anyone. Even fantasising about beating up Paul I hadn't done it that hard. It was like kicking Kelly in the face that day I got expelled from my old school – I thought I'd never do it, then I did.

It would've been easy later, but I didn't get the chance.

Chrissie screeched louder, nearly bursting my eardrums. Then someone hauled her off and I could breathe again.

I shook later, in my room. It had been mad doing that, mental. Chrissie fucking deserved it but now she'd kill me. I thought tactics. If I went to Rocky's every day after school then came back late, she couldn't get near me—

I held my phone. He didn't text.

He didn't text on Sunday morning either, or the afternoon.

I cried a bit.

Later I was starving so I needed to go down to tea. I unlocked my bedroom door. I opened it slow, slow, peeking out in case Chrissie was there ready to slit my throat. Then

I locked the door from the outside in case she got in and took a shit on my bed. It's the sort of thing she'd do.

Petesy and Darren ignored me. They sat with Chrissie, all giving me dirty looks. I gave dirty looks back. But it was still shit.

I checked the phone, back in my room. Nothing. There was nothing on the telly. I didn't want to read. I lay for ages, staring at the wall. I was so bored I went to bed early.

He didn't text.

2.

I say, —That's four forty five— and I take the fiver and I give the customer 55p from my stash under the till. I crumple the fiver in my fist and when the customer's away and Niall's not looking, I put the fiver in my jeans pocket. Easy as fuck and I can't believe I used to shag fellas for it.

I wear my jeans now to the shop instead of my trackie bottoms, cos the pockets are better. It's piss easy, this, I just have to be all casual putting the money in my pocket, sort of waving my hand over my pocket and not digging in. If Niall sees me he might just think I'm scratching my fanny, and he'll be so he'll never look near me again.

I've been waiting months for today cos it's Christmas Eve and I'm off for a week now and I had it all planned to get pissed every day. But now it's here, I don't want to be off work, cos I've only nuck seventy quid so far. Seventy five now with this fiver. It's better than a poke up the hole but it's still shite, it's nowhere near enough. And there's no chance of not going ahead, I think it'd send me mad to give this all up now.

It's piss easy putting the money in my pocket once I have it in my fist, but it's fucking hard getting the money in the first place. It'd be no probs in a shop like some of the ones back home, like a mobile van that's not even a shop and doesn't have a till. But everything's scanned here, even like a 2p sweet, cos the till has to open for change. So I can't just lift money cos then the float will be short at the end of the day.

But I figured it out, I'm maybe not as thick as I think. Here's what I do. I stash change now from my own money, coppers and silver and the odd quid or two from bus fares or the offy. I hide it under the till, on the shelf behind my Coke tin, so I can get to it easy when the till's open.

I wait til someone buys something nearly a fiver or a tenner. (I had twenty once, from a man who came in like his arse was on fire and bought our biggest box of chocolates, wonder what he did). And then I just… don't put the purchase through the till. I give them change from the stash and I keep the note they give me. I've got a story all ready about the till not working, in case someone asks.

Only one person's ever said anything about it, yesterday that was. She was a nurse from the hospital across the road, a fat frowny bitch wanting a fight. She was a bitch, cos it was fuck all to do with her.

—The till doesn't look broken to ME, she said. —It looks like it's ON—

She was smug, pouncey, the way some people are when they think they've caught you out, even if it's no skin off their nose. And I didn't know I knew this word but I must've heard it somewhere, I said, — The till's on, but it's malfunctioning. (I've just been down to the office to ask Gemma how to spell malfunctioning. She's all impressed.)

I'm lucky near the end of this last shift cos someone buys a tin of Quality Street at £9.99 special offer before Christmas. I give him 1p from my stash and I slide the tenner into my pocket. Eighty five now. Seven, eight weeks. Maybe.

3.

Chrissie and Petesy and Darren were best buds and the three musketeers the next morning. They lounged against the wall while Linda started the minibus, looking over at me and laughing.

Chrissie was hyper and loud, in her most annoying mood. She screeched so loud Linda nearly drove off the road, cos Chrissie was in the seat right behind her.

—That's enough, Chrissie! Linda shouted.

I smirked so Chrissie could see. I threw her a dirty look. But she just stared right back at me. Like trying to decide the best way to kill me, should she stab me or drop me off a high bridge – and she put her finger across her throat and drew it back to say I was dead.

I didn't let on, but I was shitting myself a bit now. Chrissie's different from Kelly at my last school. She's a proper psycho instead of Kelly who just tried to act like it. Chrissie could push me down the stairs easy, and be all innocent and open-mouthed that I was wearing slippy shoes.

I had to keep away.

When we got into school Chrissie said to Petesy and Darren, —See youse LATER, and looked at me, all Full of Meaning. She was probably talking shite, but still, I'd figure something out for lunchtime so she couldn't find me—

She'd have everyone in our class on side, I thought, the way Nicola did in our old school when the two of us fell out. But she didn't get a chance, not right away anyway, cos when we walked into our form room everyone gasped cos of her bloodshot eye. This fella Simon shouted out, — Here Chrissie, who gave you the shiner?

She'd say me, she'd say it was Lisa what dun it, so they'd all feel sorry for her, poor bullied Chrissie. But she didn't. She was blocked and she fell, she said.

—Fell on what, your fella's fist? Simon went, and everyone laughed. I hadn't thought of that, people thinking it was a fella. But it was good, cos it was more scundering for her. Maybe she should've said it was me.

He didn't text. And then I'd no phone.

We were in history. Me and Chrissie still had to sit beside each other cos the teacher was Schizo McCullough and he went mental if anyone changed seats. My phone beeped. A text, Rocky had texted—

But I sat dead still and quiet. McCullough went mental too if he caught anyone using their phone outside break times. All the other teachers cracked up about that too but he did it properly, he went bug-eyed and red. But I couldn't wait. It must be Rocky cos no-one else had my number. Maybe the text was about seeing me later.

I put my bag on my lap. I put my hand inside, like maybe I was getting a pen. I closed my hand around the phone and flipped it open.

Chrissie shouted out.

—Sir, Lisa's using her phone—

McCullough came over so fast it was like he was on skates. Faster than Paul even, when Paul used to barrel across the room like a thumpy ninja.

Schizo McCullough took my phone.

—You can have this at home time, Miss O'Neill—

He put the phone, MY phone, in his pocket.

Chrissie's smugness was like a force field.

I'd kill her.

After last bell I was up like a pin was jabbed in my arse. I bolted to the history room but McCullough wasn't there. The staff room, he'd be in the staff room—

I slowed down in the main corridor cos running makes my tits bounce and fellas make fun of me, but I walked fast to the staff room corridor. That was the same corridor for the front door out to the car park, so Chrissie, Petesy and Darren leaned against the wall watching me.

—The minibus'll be here in a minute, Chrissie said. She didn't say it to be nice, she said it to be bossy.

—I know! I snarled over my shoulder. —I'll be back in a minute—

McCullough gave me my phone back, making me listen to stuff first about classrooms not being bear gardens and if everyone used their phones in class then where would we be. The text was from Rocky.

how r u, it said. What did that mean, *how r u*? Did he want to see me? What did I text back?

I was back at the front door before seeing Chrissie and Petesy and Darren weren't there any more. The minibus had left without me.

I rang Rocky without thinking about it, cos my phone was open in my hand. And his voice went, —Hi there! and he sounded surprised and pleased. —What's up?

So I told him.

—What? he said, all shocked, —they've left you there?

I said yeah. My voice went small. My eyes felt small too.

—Hang on, he said, —I'll come and get you.

4.

He turned up in a tiny green car looking like it hadn't been washed since it was born. He roared into the car park like he owned it. He beeped the horn. I went over fast before the teachers came out.

Raymie was in the back. He flashed his brown teeth and waved a spliff. I got in and Rocky roared off.

—Raymie came along for the ride, Rocky said, shouting, cos the car engine was like a helicopter. Raymie grinned and waved the spliff again.

—Do you like our car? Rocky said. —Me and Raymie chipped in for it, it was only a hundred quid each—

So he wasn't skint after buying me the phone, that was good. Raymie passed me the spliff, and after a couple of draws I thought fuck Chrissie and all the rest.

Rocky drove to the flats, then Raymie jumped into the driver's seat of the car and roared off. I was glad, I just wanted Rocky.

I was a bit scundered, but, cos Rocky had never seen me in my school uniform and I was fat and wild-haired in it. But it didn't matter, cos as soon as we were in the flat he said,

—Didn't want to say in front of Raymie, but you're looking sexy there in your school uniform, babe—

Then he said, laughing,—It's a bit sick I know, but I can't help it—

Then he said, all serious,

—So what happened?

I told him. He said Chrissie and Petesy and Darren were cunts and so were the social workers. He held me on the couch in a hug. Maybe he'd want a shag. I'd rather stay like this, but I didn't mind really, and he'd come and got me when everyone had left me—

But he didn't. It was nearky like he wanted rid of me. He said,

—Well I suppose we should get you home—

—I don't want to, I said. My voice was small again and I hated it cos it was whiny like a baby. But I didn't want to. I didn't want be at the gulag or school or anywhere apart from that flat.

He looked concerned then. Proper concerned, not like the social workers only letting on. He said,

—I've the car now. Maybe we can head away for a couple of days, just us two?

It was the best thing I'd heard since Chrissie's eye popping under my finger. We could go miles away, where no-one knew us, maybe Donegal or down south, like I'd left the gulag and was away forever—

I didn't know it'd come out til it did.

—Not just for a couple of days, I said. —I want to head away properly, never come back—

I'd never said before this was my long-term Cunning Plan, that I was only in the gulag til I could leave again. I was only there still cos I had to save up, and wait til it got warmer cos I'd probably sleep outside at first.

But by then… I didn't want to go on my own. It'd be brilliant having someone with me. And Rocky would be even better than Chrissie or another girl cos he was a fella, and older. He'd look after me and not let fellas in squats say I was ugly.

And anyway, I didn't want to be away from him now.

So I told him. I said I wouldn't go if he didn't, I wouldn't go on my own.

He said nothing. He thought about it. I sweated. He said,

—Yeah. Why the fuck not. C'mon do it—

I squealed and threw my arms around him.

—Give me a few weeks, sort out some money? he said.

No bother from me. Waiting was tickety boo cos then we'd be away, me and Rocky away from everyone.

I'd still get Chrissie back for leaving me stranded. I lay on my bed smoking, thinking how. I'd put shite in her dinner or I'd push her down the stairs or I'd piss in her bed — but I'd get her back. And then? I'd leave and I'd never see her again.

5.

It's my third Christmas in the hostel. It's all right. The staff make Christmas dinner for everyone and there's loads of sweets and cakes still left from all the donations. And I've two big bottles of cider in my room for later.

It's only two fellas and Debbie and me here today, apart from the staff. Me and Debbie take over the TV in the living room, cos the fellas always get their own way so they can go and fuck. Gemma's on shift, she tells us stuff about her boyfriend. She moans about him not doing the dishes and it makes me feel like an old old woman. I think, oh the things I could tell you.

I don't, course I don't.

I'm back up in my room now. I loaded a plate with sandwiches and cake, and I'm writing this and watching telly, and I'm getting pissed and smoking out the window. It's been an all right day.

I'm going to tell it now, tell it all. Well, what I can, some I won't write. I've got this week off and if I can't nick stuff from the shop to help me then I'm going to write instead, write til my hand hurts. It hasn't helped at all yet but maybe it will.

6.

I lay on the chilled pissy floors of the boys' toilets. My face was wet. The blood in my mouth tasted like copper.

I thought I'd kill her. But Chrissie got there first.

I thought Chrissie's payback for her bloodshot eye was getting the minibus to leave without me that day – she told Joanne I was at the drama club and Mr McCullough was going to drive me back to the gulag. I was stupid again, thinking that would be the end of it. A bloodshot eye was a bigger revenge, I should've knew that. I should've remembered Chrissie was a psycho.

It was the day after the minibus, lunchtime. We'd PE before, so I planned for after. I'd change back into my uniform fast, so I'd get to the canteen first and get a seat before Chrissie, Petesy and Darren. So I didn't circle with my tray while they laughed at me. They did it the day before and other people laughed at me too, and I ate my lunch with a burning face trying to make myself tiny.

I should've gone to the library to stay out of their way, but I was starving and I wanted chips. So I stampeded to the changing rooms when Connolly blew her whistle and I was in the shower and out and dried and ready to get dressed in about a minute.

My tights were gone.

I looked under the bench, and in my PE bag, and in my schoolbag and even in my coat pocket in case someone was taking the piss. But I knew the tights were away. And I knew it was Chrissie, she'd hid them or nicked them or chopped them up into bits. She wouldn't give them back even if I cried and begged, and I couldn't say anything to Connolly cos that was touting. I was no tout even if Chrissie was.

I let on nothing was wrong. I could feel Chrissie near me, darting looks and bubbling with laughter, but after I pulled my jumper over my head she was gone.

I fiddled with my PE bag, just making, til everyone went out chattery for lunch. Then I looked everywhere for my tights, even the bog cubicles and the kit cupboard and back in the gym. But I knew they were gone. Fucking bitch.

I put my PE socks on instead. I looked like a dick and my legs were milk bottle white and everyone would laugh. I couldn't go to the canteen. I wouldn't get a seat, and people would look at my legs and go why's she wearing them socks is she special needs.

I'd go to the library.

I went out of the changing rooms and along the next corridor.

I sort of knew I was passing the fellas' bogs cos I could smell the piss from ages away, but I thundered along thinking of Chrissie chopped up into pieces. The door of the bogs opened. There was a flash of person. Someone grabbed me, hauled me. I fell into the bathroom with my skirt flying up. I fell onto the stinky boypiss tiles. I maybe hit my head. I don't remember.

I knew it was Chrissie even before I saw her pink and white sparkly trainers in front of me. Fuck it. Fuck her. If she wanted a fight she'd fucking get one. But then, more feet, bigger ones. Petesy and Darren.

I was dead. I got up, slow, playing for time. They all watched.

Chrissie laughed, she'd got me. Darren moved in front of the door.

—Told you I'd get you, Chrissie said.

—Aye, three against one, Chrissie, you're a big fucking woman aren't you, I snapped. She, they, couldn't know I was scared. It's always worse if people know you're scared—

She laughed again. A soft, easy, laugh, the sort people do when they have all the control.

She stepped forward. There was a flurry of school uniform and hair and then she was on me and either Petesy or Darren were too and I was on the floor. I fought back but there was no point. This wasn't a fight. Even if I beat her that was why Petesy and Darren were there, to jump on—

Her weight was on me. Her hair was in my mouth. She knelt on my arms. Someone stood on my legs. It hurt, it fucking hurt, I screamed I couldn't help it—

She hit me. She ripped a chunk of my hair out. She hit me, and I couldn't move or fight back cos of Chrissie's knees on my arms and either Petesy or Darren's feet on my legs. It was proper punching, right in the face, like Paul used to. I'd thought at least being in the gulag all that was over. It hurt, it fucking hurt—

I tried to get away but moving hurt my arms under her knees. My arms were numb and my fingers were like they'd drop off. She hit me and hit me and hit me. Fuck pretending I wasn't scared, I started shouting, someone might hear me even if they were all in the canteen miles away. I tasted blood.

She put her hand over my mouth, her fat sweaty hand tasting of salt. She shouted.

—Petesy, Darren!

As she leaned over me she watched with those glittery piggy eyes. She kept her hand over my mouth. Whoever had been on my legs jumped off and then Petesy and Darren's trainers were beside me. I heard the boys laugh and jeer as Chrissie leaned over more, more, and let a big slabbery spit hang over my face, above my eyes.

I whipped my head to the side even though there was no point, I was pinned under her and anyway my trying to get away made her shriek laughing.

The slabber dripped on my face. It was minging, gross, worse than *stuff* or periods, I was going to boke, it ran down my cheek, it'd go into my ear—

She hissed, —Hurry up before someone comes in!

And, upside down from the cold pissy floor, I saw Petesy and Darren pull the zips of their trousers down.

Were they going to piss on me? Were they going to shag me, was that why Chrissie stole my tights, to make it easier for them—

—Hurry up! she said again, laughing now, and she moved back a bit out of their way, but still on me, and I could see them, pumping their dicks in their fists and they were wanking, wanking over me. But maybe that was only them getting ready, maybe they'd stick it in my mouth, maybe they'd rip my knickers off—

Chrissie shrieked and jumped to the side.

It landed on me.

I tried to get up but Chrissie kicked me in the head.

It landed on me again.

They laughed, they laughed, and I lay there with their *stuff* dripping over me, down me, in my hair—

Chrissie leaned down to my face. She nearly whispered it.

—I SAID you were a slut, Lisa O'Neill, she said.

The door banged and they were gone.

7.

I couldn't move. And I thought about just staying there, on that pissy tile floor. I wanted to stay there always. But then, what if someone came in? Saw me there like that all blood and tears and stuff? What would they do to me in the fellas' bogs – on their turf and on my own?

I sat up, slow. I tried to do a deep breath but a sob came out instead. Things hurt, my face and my arms and my chest, but fuck that. It was in my hair, I could feel it in my hair—

It was on my jumper as well. A bit on my skirt and another bit – boke – on my leg. I rubbed it off with the end of my jumper sleeve. I heaved doing it. Sick came up and I swallowed it down.

(You're good at swallowing aren't you, Rocky says you are, maybe you ARE a slut Lisa O'Neill–)

My face was sticky. If there was *stuff* on it I'd definitely boke. But when I dipped a fingertip into the sticky and looked with my eyes half shut, it was blood.

I got up — it took me two goes — and staggered over to the tap. I looked all over me, wiping blood off where I could see it. I scrubbed at my hair.

Voices, outside. People out of lunch. I had to get out of there—

I ran down the corridor. But to where? And my head said right away, *Rocky's*.

But he couldn't see me in that state.

I went to the receptionist's office.

—I fell, I said.

I said it to the receptionist and I said it to Joanne when she came to get me. I'd fell in the girls' toilets and now I felt sick and I wanted to go home.

Joanne tried to get me to talk, cos it would've been obvious even to a six year old with a white stick that someone had battered me. —Is someone bullying you, Lisa, is that it? she said. —If you want to tell me something it won't go any further—

Bollocks it wouldn't. And then the next time Chrissie got me it'd have been even worse.

Up in my room, I stared in the mirror.

My hair was like I'd been electrocuted, a chunk of it was missing at the top. There was blood under my nose. Blood on my top lip and between my teeth too, I looked like Dracula. My face looked all scraped and bulgy, so there'd be bruises later, I'd had that before. Chrissie would laugh. They all would. They'd see me and remember and they'd laugh—

I boked in the sink.

I pulled my clothes off and wrapped a towel around me. I shivered. I sort of forgot where I was for a couple of seconds, like fainting but awake. *Why were my clothes off? For a shower, I was taking a shower.* So I needed my shower gel, it was in my PE bag—

I held the bottle and it was still wet. I felt spaced. I thought, cos when I last held this shower gel Chrissie was going through my stuff. Taking my tights. All so I'd be late for lunch and she could lie in wait with Petesy and Darren—

I was sick again.

I scrubbed them off me in the shower but I stayed for ages after. I leaned against the glass, the water beating down on me. I was so tired. So knackered. My head wouldn't stop. They'd be home soon, the three of them. They'd be in the same place as me and they'd jeer at me in the dining room.

I couldn't see them again, I knew I couldn't lay eyes on them. I was nearly sick again just at the thought. Cos even if they didn't laugh at me, they still knew. They'd seen me, there on the tiles.

I was going to Rocky's.

And then I thought, maybe I could go somewhere else. I could leave for good. Go off on my own. Get to Belfast or even Dublin and then to London where no-one would ever find me. Where no-one knew me.

But that'd be stupid. Rocky had a flat, and drink, and he'd hug me after he shagged me. He was the only person I could talk to.

I texted him, back in my room. It took a couple of goes cos my fingers felt too big. I texted *u in can I call over*. And he texted back right away, saying *yeah*.

But Raymie was there too.

8.

I was meant to text Rocky when I got to the block of flats, but a fella was leaving just as I arrived so I slipped in the door before it banged shut. Rocky's flat door was open as well. So I saw them before they saw me. They were on the floor in a cloud of smoke. They were watching a porno.

I couldn't tell Rocky now, not with someone there. It wouldn't be the whole story anyway, course it wouldn't, but I could say at least Chrissie got them to gang up on me and the three of them gave me a kicking—

I thought I'd wait til Raymie left then I'd tell Rocky after. But when both of them heard me come in and turned round, I didn't have to open my mouth.

Rocky jumped up.

—Fuck, what happened you?

I started to talk but then I was crying. I was still in the doorway of the living room. It took a minute before I said it.

—Chrissie and Petesy and Darren jumped me—

Rocky and Raymie shook their heads and said Chrissie and Petesy and Darren were cunts.

—Come on, babe, come in, Rocky said. He put his arm around me and drew me inside the room.

The porno was still on. It was a bit weird but I didn't really care. I just wanted someone to say I'd be all right. I wanted someone to say a wrong was done to me, and it was wrong.

—Do you want us to sort it out? Rocky said.

—What, I said, —beat the three of them up?

They looked at each other. Rocky said,

—Well no, not the fellas, cos Chrissie started it, she got them to do it didn't she?

But it was the fellas who wanked over me, I thought, fast before I could stop. But I didn't say it. And anyway Rocky was right wasn't he. Chrissie got Petesy and Darren to do it. So I said,

—Well, like what?

They looked at each other again. Raymie grinned. Rocky said,

—My cock down her throat would soon shut her fucking fat mouth—

Well, yeah. Maybe. It'd serve her fucking well right.

Raymie went out for chips. When the front door banged shut Rocky said, —C'mere—

He pulled me towards him. He hugged me and he kissed me.

—You're brave, he said, —you're a brave girl—

I nearly melted. He hugged me hard and I was happy, warm and happy. But then his hand was on my head. He pushed his tracksuit bottoms down. He pushed my head down.

I pulled away. I said, —But Raymie'll be back in a minute—

—Ah come on, he said. —Sure you've got me started now—

I did it.

—Good girl, he said.

He pulled his bottoms back up. I swigged my beer, deep. I'd never get used to the taste, the burn, I thought.

I never did.

Raymie brought vodka back along with the chips. Thank fuck, cos it was time to forget.

—Here Lisa, Raymie said, —you have first swig—

I cracked the bottle open and necked. I nearly choked but I kept going, big slugs til my eyes watered.

—Fuck, you needed that, Raymie said. He grinned from his brown teeth.

But I had the buzz off it already, so I grinned back. He smiled again, and winked.

Rocky didn't see.

Rocky said,

—Here Lisa, will we stick the porno back on?

He was rolling a spliff, not looking at either of us. Like he'd said does anyone want tea. Was he on glue! Course I didn't want to watch porno with Raymie there! And what if a waxed woman came on and Rocky said to Raymie, Lisa got that done on Saturday herself?

I didn't have to say I didn't want to. Cos Raymie laughed. He said, —Fuck's sake Rocky, course she doesn't want to. The wee girl's scundered—

I smiled at him again, over Rocky's head. He winked at me again, so I looked away fast in case I was being a slut. But it was nice, him winking at me. Knowing someone fancied me, it was the first time in my life someone had said that about me.

I had Rocky too. My boyfriend. So fuck Chrissie and all the rest of them. They hadn't a clue. They were kids.

Raymie went out again when the vodka was nearly done. He was bouncy when he came back. He threw a tiny plastic bag onto the wooden crate.

—Here we go now, he said. —Let's get the party staaaaaaarted!

—What is it? I said.

—Coke, Raymie and Rocky said.

Rocky said, —Want to try some?

Course I fucking did, was he thick? Everyone went on about coke by then, especially Chrissie who was nearly in rehab by the way she got on. I'd had E loads but I'd never tried coke. So course I said yeah.

Rocky and Raymie grinned.

—That's a girl, Rocky said.

I watched as Raymie picked up the bag up and knocked powder from it onto a CD case. This was brilliant. It was like the first time I took E, just the thought of it and knowing I'd do it and here it was, here it was now. It was class, it was proper drugs.

—Card, Raymie said. Rocky dug in his pocket and found his national insurance card. Raymie mashed the powder flat with it, then smoothed it into lines (chopping, that's called).

Rocky rolled up a fiver. He passed it to me.

—Ladies first—

I knew how to take coke cos of TV. I was a bit pissed now too, so I took the fiver like I'd done this a million times. Like a supermodel at a nightclub. I pushed the fiver up one nostril and leaned over the CD case. My hair fell in my face but Rocky laughed and held it back. I knew him and Raymie were grinning over the top of my head but I didn't care. It wasn't a bad grin, I could feel it.

When I sniffed there was nothing, I didn't feel anything. The line was still on the CD case, untouched. Rocky and Raymie fell about laughing.

—You need to hold the other side of your nose shut, Rocky said, —so it goes up the side you're snorting from—

So I did. I did a huge sniff and it was like in primary school when Melissa Connolly dared me to smell the mustard jar on the teachers' table in the dining hall, and I didn't know about mustard so I took the biggest sniff I could and I thought my head was going to lift off. Everyone laughed then the way Rocky and Raymie laughed now. It wasn't a laugh against me, it was cos it was funny.

My eyes watered, watching Rocky and Raymie laugh. I didn't care, it was fucking funny. I clapped my nose and said Fuck. They laughed more. There was a stinking taste down my throat, like blowjobs but mediciney as well, like crushed paracetamol. I coughed.

—Drippage, Rocky said, and Raymie said, —Don't worry you'll get used to it.

Later it was brilliant, like I could do anything. Like my first E, when I was off my face but more than that I was so happy to be away from Paul and my ma. Now I was with Rocky, and we were going away soon. He'd said.

—Take me away from all this, I said to Rocky like an old black and white film, swooning against him and laughing like a mental. Him and Raymie laughed, we'd been laughing for hours by then.

Rocky said, —You're mad, wee girl, but I love you anyway—

It wasn't like I. Love. You, I knew that. He wouldn't say that with Raymie there. He meant he loved how I was, all giggly and silly. But still. It was the first time anyone said it to me. The first time anyone said they liked me, even, cos me and Nicola and the rest didn't go around saying I like you or stuff like that.

So it was partly cos of that, when Rocky said again about putting the porno back on. And cos of the coke and feeling like a model in a nightclub, maybe. So this time I said, —Yeah. Why not.

—Good girl, Rocky said, and I was.

Raymie chopped more lines. We snorted them. Rocky put the porno on again.

We were all on the floor. Rocky put his arm round me. Then he threw the blanket over us both. Raymie was behind us, his foot near my shoulder.

I was warm so I took my boots and socks off and lay down again, my toes sticking out from under the blanket. One of my feet jittered, maybe cos of the coke. I tried to stop it but it wouldn't so I looked at the porno. It was a fella and two girls again. Maybe all porno is a fella and two girls, I didn't know—

One of the girls sort of writhed around the fella. She kissed and licked his neck and chest with that sort of hungry look girls do in films when they're trying to look sexy.

But it worked. She did look sexy. I wondered could I do it.

The other girl writhed around the fella too. The camera went down, cos she was giving him a blowjob. I stared at the screen. It was a bit funny watching this with two fellas. But not like being scundered. It was like how I felt before a fight. Hyped up, like I could do anything.

Under the blanket, Rocky's hand touched the button of my jeans. I lifted my head up fast, cos of Raymie. But Rocky smiled and nodded it was OK, so I sneaked a look behind me. Raymie was watching the porno and not us. So I lay down again. It didn't matter, Raymie wouldn't see, and even if he did so what—

My jeans button snapped open. Rocky's hand was there, inside my knickers. He rubbed me, where I was smooth from the waxing.

Then it – something – happened in my brain. My head roared like a lion inside, all the coke and the vodka and the porno blasting me like a fucking train, and I wanted to grab Rocky and pull him down on me. I wanted to FUCK him. My head had never said that before, about anyone. I wanted to do it, to him, even with Raymie there—

I was a slut, like Chrissie said. Cos Raymie was there, and he might watch, and my head roared again like SO FUCKING WHAT. Like a jolt in my head, like an explosion of fuck it.

My body jolted too, all the way from where Rocky rubbed at me right down to my feet. I wriggled round for a better angle and he pushed his fingers inside me. Raymie could see, must be able to see, but my head hollered I don't give a fuck, I want this, doing this and doing everything, being this and being everything.

Rocky pushed the blanket off us. He grabbed at me. He pushed my jeans and knickers down. The air was cold around my body but I lay on the floor anyway, like an exhibit, like a painting. Raymie could see, could see all of me, and I didn't fucking care. I was shy but excited at the same time. Like anything could happen and anything should.

—Nice, someone said. Rocky or Raymie, I didn't know, but I knew it was about my waxing.

Rocky stroked it, the smoothness of it. I writhed a bit, cos who gave a fuck who was watching? Chrissie and the social workers and the fucking Pope could have been there and I wouldn't have given a shit—

—Givvis a look? Raymie said.

—All right, Rocky said.

They were over me. Raymie put his hand out to touch, pulled it back, put it out again. I laughed. He was like a timid kid.

I pushed my hips towards him. I let him touch. He stroked me.

I was like a sex goddess. I was so strong.

I smiled up at Rocky, all strong and sexy. He sat me up. He pulled my jumper off. He unsnapped my bra. He laid me down again on the cold cold floor.

I lay there, loving it. Loving them looking at me like I was a queen, and if Chrissie could see me now.

Rocky's hand went to his tracksuit bottoms. He pushed them down. He shuffled closer to me. He stared, like daring me to say something, but I nodded from the floor. A girl went Oh Oh Oh on the porno and it mixed with the thumping in my ears. Was I doing this? Was I about to shag my boyfriend in front of another fella?

And then Rocky was on me and pushing into me, hard, and it hurt but it didn't matter, cos I could take it good as anyone. He did it to me and I lay there, taking it, how he liked me to. My shoulders slid up and down on the bare floor.

Rocky looked up. I followed his look to Raymie. Raymie who stood over us, watching. Raymie who had his hand down his jeans, stroking his dick.

Raymie looked down at me. Slow and deliberate, he pushed his jeans down. I saw him. I saw HIM. He was big, like Rocky. Maybe even bigger.

Rocky kept doing it to me and I kept looking up at Raymie.

Raymie knelt down, right beside me. I didn't care. They could do what they wanted. The porno was still on, but I was better – I was live.

My head was twisted round, something, Raymie's dick, shoved into my mouth. What the fuck! my head went, but then I caught on and I did it like Rocky had showed me.

Rocky pulled out, and I was flipped over onto my knees and he was pushing into me from behind. We'd never done it like that before and it was deep, it was sore, but I couldn't cry out cos Raymie was back in my mouth. Maybe I'd bitten off more than I could chew (haha) but like I was going to stop now or like I even could. I wasn't a prick teaser.

I heard Rocky coming and then he slipped out of me, wet and loose. And I heard him say to Raymie, —Sloppy seconds?

I got what Rocky wanted. I wanted to do it, mostly. I was still a sex goddess, cos of the coke, and Raymie fancied me and Rocky looked after me so it was only fair.

So when Raymie pulled me onto my back again I let him.

9.

—What's that on your arms? he says.

And I seize up.

Me and Niall's sort of going out. I don't know if I want to, but I've sort of drifted into it cos I don't know what else to say if he says do I fancy coming over.

We're in his flat. In bed. It's the third of January, my first day back after Christmas. I've got a hundred and five quid now, over a sixth of the way. I see it in my head like a pie, with one slice coloured in.

Niall's never seen my arms, cos I keep my hoodie on in the shop and when we shag at the flat, I make sure it's dark or I stay under the covers. If we get up, like to roll a joint, I pull my hoodie back on and say I'm cold. So he's never seen my arms, not bare, not properly. The razor lines.

I don't give a fuck, not really. It's just I can't be fucked talking about it and seeing him do that tragic face again and then want to ask me about it. Loads of people in the hostel have scars, it's no big deal. I can't be fucked having it made a big deal.

I've got burn marks on my arms too, down towards my wrists. A splash of scar over both hands. A spread on both arms. A cigarette hole on my shoulder.

A burn on my face.

So fucking what.

The burns are different. Apart from the ones on my hands and face, whivh happened when I set fire to Chrissie's skirt, the burns were done to me. I didn't mean them.

Self harm, the staff at the hostel call it. They don't get it, they can't see how it's coping. A girl from the hostel jumped off the high rise flats down the road last year. She didn't cope.

Sometimes I won't cope, I think. Like, fuck it. It's loads to put up with, inside my head and Rocky and the memories. Day after day after month after year coping with it. What's happening now, and what happened before.

Loads of people jump.

I cut my arms loads when I was in the gulag. I don't now, not as much. But sometimes. It feels the same way it did back then, it's me not jumping and the hostel staff haven't got a clue.

Debbie does it and I know why.

Niall doesn't and he'll never know why.

I move my arm under the duvet.

—*Nothing, I say.*

His look is pitying, his eyes nearly melting with concern.

—Are you all right, Lisa?

I know what'll definitely shut him up, so I go under the duvet and do it.

After, he tries to do the same on me. He's tried it before, nearly every time we shag. He dives between my legs and laps away at me, looking up at me every few seconds like a puppy all proud. Sometimes I nearly pat him on the head.

I hate it. What am I meant to do, while he does it? There's nothing I get from it, it makes me feel slabbery and gross and wound up, like a spring waiting to go off. He's trying to make me come, I know that. But I won't. I moaned a bit the first couple of times, but then he went on for ever, ages and ages. I lay there, more and more scundered and tensed up cos I didn't know how to stop him. He had the clit nearly licked off me.

He gives up. He's all hurt.

—Tell me what you like, he says. —I'm going to make you come—

He's said that before. He's a man with a mission or like he thinks he's got a magic dick.

I don't know what I like, how the fuck would I. I don't like any of it, cos again how the fuck would I. He'll not make me come, ever, I never have and I wouldn't know how.

I pull him to me again.

10.

When I woke up a couple of hours later in Rocky's flat, I knew I was definitely a slut.

I was on the floor, cold, no clothes on. I pulled the blanket over me when I was conking out, I remembered doing it. But now someone was there who'd pulled most of it off.

It was Raymie. I nearly boked when I saw him. He was on his back, mouth open and slabbers coming out and his brown teeth all on show. I was like, did I let this fella shag me? And in front of my boyfriend?

I moaned, not loud in case I woke him. What the fuck was I thinking?

—It's just coke comedown, Rocky said the next day. — Everyone gets it, it's only the first couple of times—

—Is it?

What I really meant was am I a slut, but I didn't know how to ask. And when Raymie came to Rocky's flat later the three of us did it again. Rocky shagged me while I gave Raymie a blowjob and then Raymie shagged me after.

I wanted to. I can't say why I did, but it was like, well if I do it now, it's cos I want them to. Then the first time would be like I wanted to as well. It wasn't the coke and me being a slut.

—Good girl, Rocky said again after it, —good girl, you're a good girl.

11.

I didn't hear from him.

For days he didn't text. I wanted to text him but I didn't cos I was scared. He'd dumped me, I knew it. He'd dumped me for being a slut and for shagging his mate.

I cried, every night.

And the text came. It was Tuesday afternoon, late, on the minibus home. *comin over l8r??* it said. I texted back *yeah*, right away. And he texted, *i have sumthin 2 tell* u.

I didn't change my face, cos Chrissie was watching. But I went cold. He was going to dump me, I knew it. I started to shake a bit but only inside. It wasn't like I was head over heels in love or anything (well, only a bit). It was more like, if he dumps me what'll I do with myself? Who'll I talk to, with no friends?

I didn't care about the shagging. It's only fellas who care, so you have to let them to be with them, but I liked all the other stuff. Him hugging me and saying I was a brave girl and letting me come to his flat and being someone I could talk to. He was my first boyfriend. When I got up to my room I cried.

He waited at the door of the flats. He didn't kiss me. He said, —C'mon, and I followed him up the stairs.

When we got inside he pulled me down onto the couch and kissed me. He mustn't be dumping me, I thought, so when he pushed my head down I did it like I loved it.

He rolled a spliff, after. He didn't say anything. I waited but the silence stretched more and more til I could nearly hear it. So I said, small, —So what do you have to tell me?

—What? he said like he didn't know, like he didn't remember. I said it again.

He rolled the spliff. He licked the papers. He said,

—The peelers came round yesterday, about you—

Stuff dropped in my stomach.

I whispered,

—Why?

—Cos of you being here. Cos of you being late back to the home a couple of times. They wanted to talk to me, cos they said you're only fourteen and you're underage—

I'm fifteen now, I nearly said but didn't, cos I'd been too scundered to tell anyone it was my birthday, cos it's like fishing for a present, and anyway I couldn't see why it mattered, why the peelers cared what fucking age I was—

I didn't say anything. I let Rocky tell me.

—They think I'm a paedo, h said. —They were asking do we have sex and what do we do and am I your boyfriend—

He said,

—So I said no—

And I nearly cried. I knew he had to say that, but still.

—I had to, he said. —They were being real cunts, like does she come here of her own accord or do you get her to come over. And if the lift me I'll get killed in jail for being a paedo—

My heart tumbled. Why hadn't I thought of that, why. He'd get beat up, stabbed—

He wasn't going to dump me but he might get lifted, cos of me, and then he was dead.

I said,

—So what are we going to do?

He didn't pause. He said right away,

—Well, it's like you said, isn't it? We'll have to leave.

12.

But it was money again, it was always money.

If I'd had money back then I'd have left the gulag the first night they put me in there. But you couldn't leave without money, you had to get food, and smokes, and drink. And even if you were good at nicking stuff you still needed money to get started, even just the bus fare to Belfast. It was always money.

Rocky said if I stayed late at the flat again like the night of the threesome the peelers would lift him for sure.

—And I want you to stay over, babe, you know I do, he said, kissing me. I leaned into him, laying my head on his chest.

Then he said,

—I know how we can get money, Saturday night—

He said we could break into a house. One with a window open, we break in and lift what we can, stuff we can sell.

I didn't know. Cos he'd get lifted for sure if we did that. Then he'd have gone to jail and got stabbed as a paedo, cos he'd broke into a house with a fourteen year old girl. I didn't care about myself, cos what could the staff or even the peelers do.

—Well, what then? he said. He was pissed off. I nearly said maybe I could do it. But he said,

—There's something else we can try—

And he said there was a fella he knew, who he owed money to. We couldn't even start saving up right now cos of this fella, cos Rocky had to pay this debt off first.

—He fancies you, Rocky said. —He'd love to shag you, I know he would—

He said,

—So I could maybe say to him he could, but he had to pay?

I said nothing. I thought about it.

Rocky said,

—And that'd clear the debt, and he might give us something else and that'd be the first of the money we need? What do you think?

I said nothing.

He said,

—I can sort some stuff during the week. We could be away by next weekend—

I didn't know. I didn't know about shagging someone I'd never seen before. I shagged fellas from the bonfire for stuff, but that was for me, money for beer and smokes. And even in the squat in Belfast, when Mackers was pimping me and I didn't know, I'd at least seen the fellas first, I'd at least thought I did it cos I wanted to.

But this would be for us. For Rocky, and for us getting away. And to keep him out of jail and not get stabbed.

It'd make me a proper slut, doing it for money like that, it was different than doing it on the spur of the moment cos I wanted some drink. But I said,

—Yeah. OK—

He'd it all planned out. I'd to meet him the next day, and we'd go into town and get some stuff.

—Like what? I said, but he said it was a surprise.

I felt like flying now I knew we'd be away, I was On Top Of The World and On Cloud Nine.

What he meant about getting some stuff was the salon, me getting another waxing. I didn't want to, but I knew by then that fellas expected it and if this fella was paying to shag me then I couldn't meet him looking like a gorilla.

This time I knew what was coming, so I dripped sweat even as I climbed onto the table with my jeans and knickers off. But I tried to be brave like Rocky liked, cos this was for us to get away.

After that, we went into a shop I didn't know, down a side street. There was lacy stuff in it, bras and knickers and stockings, red and black and hardly there. He picked up four thongs, the sort Chrissie wore. Two red and two black.

—Why're you getting me all those? I said. —We only need one, for tonight?

—Sure I like them too, he said, laughing. My face beamed red. I should've knew that, I should've bought some with my pocket money and not turned up all the time in my massive kaks. It was good he hadn't said anything—

He picked up a bra next. It was red and lacy too, and padded. (The last thing I needed was padding but I was too scundered to say.) I had to go up to the till with the bra and thongs, with money he gave me, cos he said people might think he was a paedo buying girls' underwear.

—Shoes next, he said, —then we're done—

Shoes? The fella would hardly notice shoes would he — and we'd no money anyway? But I followed Rocky to a shoe shop and he went straight for a pair. Like Chrissie had, silver with see-through glass heels and glitter, the sort of thing I'd never wear in case people laughed and said does she think she's sexy.

But they did look sexy – maybe? I nearly fell over when I stood up in them, but maybe I felt sexy in them too.

—Nice, Rocky said, —very nice—

—Shush, I said, red. But he laughed and gave me a tenner to pay.

Then he said, —Right, I've stuff to sort out, babe. So I'll see you later at the flat, all right?

—But, I said.

I stopped. We were meant to be having all day together, I wanted to say. (I didn't in case I sounded like a stalker.) But I was sad, then pissed off. Who did he think he was, fucking off on me like this? After what I'd agreed to do for us both?

I stomped through town, swinging my shopping bags. I thought about it. I'd be shagging a fella for money later. A fella I didn't know. So maybe I'd not do it. Fuck it and fuck him. The shopping bags could go in the bin and Rocky could think of something else. Maybe I'd even keep my phone, but not answer his calls any more.

I think that was the last time I could've stopped it. But I didn't.

Cos then my mind went cold. I had to have Rocky, cos I had to get away. I was going anyway, it was my plan from day one. And the only way to get money for that was to shag fellas, Chrissie told me that and she was right. And if I did it with Rocky sorting it, then he'd leave with me as well.

I'd do it.

It probably wasn't Rocky's fault, anyway. He'd have left me cos he's have had something to do.

So I wandered through town, wanting to buy myself something, but not wanting to spend any money cos we were saving up. The sooner we got away from this dump the better it'd be.

—I thought you were out for the day, Joanne said.

—No, I said, and I went upstairs to wait.

13.

I'll write it I'll write it I'll write it.

. . .

14.

I was shitting it. I staggered to Rocky's falling off the stupid shoes, and the wire of the bra digging into me and the thong cutting my arse in half. My tits bounced too, cos the bra didn't fit right in the front. I tottered along on stripper shoes and people at the precinct sniggered.

—Slut, someone said.

—Here, love, c'mere and suck my cock—

My stomach was sick and I sweated so much I could smell it even after the bath I'd just had. I told myself to wise up. It was just nerves. And it was a bit late to be all virginlike after a threesome with your boyfriend and another fella. And it wasn't like I hadn't done it before. So fuck if this fella was gross, so fucking what. Rocky'd be there and it'd only be a few minutes.

I staggered on.

It took ages to get to the block of flats. I texted Rocky when I left the gulag like he said, but he must've waited for ages cos he was pissed off.

—What kept you? he said.

He looked me up and down. He said,

—For fuck's sake, could you not have wore something a bit sexier than a pair of jeans and a jumper—

I tried to say it's all I had. But my throat choked cos of how he said it. If some random fella spoke to me like that, like a fella at school, I'd have said to fuck away off. But it's different when it's your boyfriend. Relationships have ups and downs, I knew that.

So I followed him to the flat.

It was empty.

—He'll be here in a minute, Rocky said. —Now get them clothes off so I can have a look at you—

I undressed and my face went hot. It was how he looked at me. Like measuring, like the first time seeing me.

I stood in the red thong and the red lacy bra. I shivered, but I tried to remember like having the coke. Like a sex goddess. Like the threesome was meant.

—Right, he said. —Put the shoes back on so I can see—

It was better with the shoes. I still wobbled, but I felt sexier.

—Good, he said. —Now get some vodka into you—

I sat on the couch and pulled the blanket over me, cos Rocky still looked at me in that measuring way. I swigged from the bottle, and again. And as I was just getting a buzz, the door hammered with a fist.

I nearly dropped the bottle. Rocky went out. I pulled the blanket closer. It was like being in a dream, or stoned.

Then Rocky was there with a fella. The fella was ancient, at least forty, and he was fat and had a shiny face. He looked at me, quick, then back at Rocky. He didn't look shy. He was acting like he'd come in for a drink.

What did I do now? Drop the blanket and sashay over to him and purr hello? Did he come to me?

Rocky said,

—C'mon, Lisa, for fuck's sake. Or will you sit there all night with that blanket wrapped round you—

So I let the blanket fall. I breathed deep. I got up. And I tottered over to the fella, brave and sexy.

He looked at me.

—Good tits, he said, to Rocky.

He reached out and squeezed my tits hard, honk.

—Bedroom's through there, Rocky said.

The fella took my hand. He led me out of the room.

I'd never been in Rocky's bedroom. It had a mattress with no sheets, only a sleeping bag. A stained pillow, no pillowcase. Clothes and trainers scattered on the floor.

The mattress looked stinking. Was I playing for time, maybe? Was I trying to find excuses? What did I do now, lie down or what?

The fella grabbed me. He kissed me, nearly sucking the face off me and scraping me with his stubble. He pushed me onto the mattress.

He pulled down his trousers. He climbed onto the mattress, above me.

He didn't say about a condom, and I couldn't ask cos it'd look like I was trying to get out of it. And maybe then he'd go into Rocky and say the deal's off. I had the implant anyway, Chrissie had told me about it, so it didn't matter.

He pulled my knees up. My shoes waved about behind his back, and I felt sick cos they looked so fucking stupid.

He wasn't big and it didn't hurt. It was over in a couple of minutes. After, he dabbed himself with a tissue, all fussy like his dick was made of glass. I sat up and pulled the thong back on and fixed my bra. What now? Maybe he'd kiss me again. Maybe he'd want to talk, all small talk like what was my best subjects at school—

He didn't. He didn't even look at me. He pulled his trousers up and his jumper down and he went. I waited in the room.

—Cheers, I heard him say to Rocky, and the front door banged and he must be gone.

—Good girl, Rocky said. I was on the couch, the shoes off and the blanket around my shoulders.

—Good girl, he said again.

He said,

—Would you be up for it again? If I can get someone else round?

And I said OK.

I'd done it now, so it didn't matter.

I waited in the bedroom this time, cos Rocky said it'd be easier. I waited ages. There was a knock on the front door,

Rocky's voice, talking, footsteps down the hall and another man in the room.

It was easier this time, a bit. He was older than the first fella but not as gross, and he didn't have to push me onto the mattress or haul at my thong and bra, cos I was lying down already and I'd took them off before. I kept the shoes on, cos I knew Rocky would've wanted me to.

I let the fella do it. I lay there and he did it and he climbed off and he pulled his jeans up. He went out without looking at me, same as the first one.

Then, nothing. Then, Rocky talking, probably on his phone. So that'd mean he was on his own, so I put the bra and thong on cos no way was I strolling about in the nip, and I tottered down the hall to the living room.

It was Rocky I saw first. He turned to me, something on his face I couldn't read. He wasn't on his phone.

I saw. There were three men.

They all looked at me.

They were about Rocky's age and one older, as old as the one who just left. They all looked at me, and here I was in nothing but a scrap of thong and a pair of stripper shoes and a bra that didn't even cover my tits. I crossed my arms over my chest. I tried to cross my legs, standing up. A memory flashed, Nicola having the miscarriage, standing in the squat with her knees together like a woman in a seaside postcard.

It wasn't funny. They were here for a drink, they must be. And it was Rocky's flat, so he had the right. But it was fucking shit he hadn't said, so I was stood here nearly bare—

And they were ignorant too, rude, cos they stood there, staring, getting a good look when anyone decent would've looked away. I would've looked away.

They looked at me. The silence stretched. I needed the blanket, my jeans, my jumper. But then I'd have to go past them to the couch, and they'd see my fat arse—

Rocky spoke.

—Come on, Lisa, hurry up.

Like saying, how's it going. Like saying, do you want a beer.

For a second, a long long second, I heard him wrong. There were three men here, THREE. Hurry up what? Come on what?

Like a thump in the face I got it. The men, they were part of the deal. Rocky got them round, they gave him money and they're were there to shag me—

My throat had closed and my mouth was sand, so I shook my head no. No way. Not like this, not three more—

—Lisa, Rocky said.

Firmer, Scarier. I shook my head again. Was he fucking mental, this wasn't going to happen—

He steered me away from the men looking. They'd see my arse, white and wobbling on either side of the thong.

He hissed at me.

—You said you were all right with it! You said you wanted us to get money, to get away next weekend—

And I was all right with it, wasn't I? I'd just let two old men fuck me, men I'd never seen before, I couldn't act all Victorian about it. If you shag a fella for money you can't just say straight after that your fanny's shut for the night. Not when the fellas are already there.

—C'mon, Rocky said. —Like I can tell them to fuck off after giving me the money—

He couldn't. He'd look like a dick, like under the thumb and pussywhipped and not wearing the trousers. Paul used to say that to my ma a lot, if she said something like when are you in for your tea. Stop fucking nagging me, he'd say, I'm not under anyone's fucking thumb.

That's a bad thing for fellas, I knew that, it was nearly as bad as being prick teased. And maybe Rocky would get into shit for it. Or beaten up, even, cos who knew who these men were, they could be IRA or UVF or anyone.

But three's too many, and you could've told me first, I wanted to say. I stared at him, my mouth like stuffed with dry sand.

Rocky got pissed off.

—C'mon Lisa, for fuck's sake! This is for us to get away. If you don't want to do it I'll get someone who will, no fucking problem—

I didn't want a fight. I didn't want him to dump me. And I'd have shagged all the men in the country to get away from the gulag. So I sort of shrugged, not a yes but not a no. Maybe then he'd say it didn't matter, this was mental—

He didn't.

He said, —Good. Right.

He spoke over my shoulder to the men.

—Right, he said. —Who's first?

And the men took me into the bedroom. And they did it to me one by one, and it was black and dark and sore and terrible even with the coke they rubbed on my gums before they started.

I see it now, like from above. A man on top of me and two watching, silently, passing a wrap of coke back and forth. My eyes are closed, cos it's so terrible, them watching, I can't even describe it. So scundering, like people seeing you on the bog. So I closed my eyes, and I screwed up my face, and I remember I had *hurry up hurry up* banging over and over in my head.

The third one didn't like me closing my eyes when he was in me. He gripped my face, digging his fingers in. He made me look. It was the worst of the three cos he looked demented. He stared straight in my face like his eyes would bulge out of his head. Tears came into my eyes. He stared at me and smiled.

15.

—See, Rocky said, —it wasn't that bad was it—

I had my jeans and jumper on again. I sat on the couch, wrapped in the blanket cos I couldn't get warm. Maybe cos the mattress had been cold, with no covers on it—

I swallowed the memory down with the vodka, and again.

—That's eighty quid we made, Rocky said, —and I can probably get fifty or sixty in the week, so we should be able to head off next Saturday. Sunday at the latest—

I nodded, not feeling it. As long as we got way, and soon. A hundred and thirty or forty quid was loads. We could sleep in the car. A hundred and thirty or forty quid was ages, weeks.

—I might be able to get more, he said. —It depends on this deal I have on during the week—

He was businesslike and I didn't like it. He should have held me, I thought, say I'd done well and been really brave and everything was all right. He should have said I was a good girl.

But he didn't. He said,

—You nearly fucked it up there, you know, acting like you didn't want to—

The room wavered on me when he said that, swear to fuck it was like it moved. I couldn't see properly, I could hardly hear. Just pulsing, and his voice coming at me.

—Do you want me kneecapped? Rocky said. —One of those fellas is UVF—

The room wavered again. I'd knew it, I'd knew that last fella was dodgy, I knew he was a psycho—

—Sorry, I said.

He didn't hear, cos my voice was too small.

And then he said it. He might have some other fellas interested, so we could get a couple of men round again if I was up for it.

—Tomorrow night? Then I'll sort a couple of deals in the week and we can go first thing Saturday—

He saw me hesitate. He saw me shake. He got pissed off again.

—Do you want us to break into a house instead, is that it?

—No—

But I had to say it. Even if he dumped me — no not now he couldn't — I had to say it. The first two fellas I'd coped with, cos it'd been just us in the room. But with the three all at once—

I looked at the floor so he couldn't see me crying.

I said, —But not loads of fellas at a time, just one—

—Aye all right all right! he said. —Are you doing it or not?

My voice was from away. It echoed in my ears, like after being in the pool.

—OK, I said.

16.

He said come over at seven.

I wore the bra and the shoes and another thong, a new one cos the three men before ripped the other off me. I hoped Rocky wouldn't shout at me for wearing my jeans and jumper again, cos I'd nothing else.

I could still hardly walk in the stripper shoes, but I left the gulag early to get there in time.

He waited for me at the door.

It was one fella, like Rocky promised. But the fella wanted a blowjob not a shag, and he nearly choked me. I gagged and cried but he went faster. My eyes were like popping out with panic, I couldn't breathe.

When he finished he looked down at me like a town he'd conquered.

—That's ninety we have now, Rocky said after the fella left. —We'll definitely have enough to go by Saturday, I'm getting more money this week—

He saw my look.

—It'll be next Saturday at the latest, babe, he said. —Less than a week. I promise.

I could hardly stop grinning all week. We had the money! We were going!

I planned stuff like a ninja, I was good at that. We needed food cos then our money would last longer, so I did a sneaky nosy in the kitchen on the Tuesday evening. I let on to speak to Jean, but really I was having a quick duke at the shelves and the larder to see what food was there and if I could nick any to stretch our money further when we went.

There was loads of bread, and tins of beans, and a big packet of ham when Jean opened the fridge. I'd have to get into the kitchen on the Saturday morning.

I remembered leaving for Belfast, months ago by then. I remembered planning this as a kid, sneaking money from

Paul's jeans, putting away matches and tins over weeks. And the peelers bringing me back for Paul to beat me up. I was an old hand at leaving, I could give classes.

It'd never worked out for me so far, but it would this time. I could feel it. This one was permanent.

17.

I got into shit at school.

I got suspended.

And I knew if I went back I was dead.

It wasn't Chrissie this time. Well it sort of was, cos she was the one said in the first place about me shagging Rocky. So there were sniggers all the time about me being a slut, going out with an old age pensioner, I'd fuck anything that moved—

This fella Simon was worst. He was in my form class, the fella who'd said to Chrissie about falling into her boyfriend's fist. He'd say things. *Oh I'd LOVE a blowjob*, and, *I never get shags, maybe cos I'm not an OAP—*

I let on to ignore him but my eyes were tight and hot, not crying.

It was the Wednesday it happened, two days before Rocky's. We lined up for assembly and there was something, someone, at me. Not touching but close.

I spun round.

Simon was right behind me, thrusting right at me, holding his hands like shagging me from behind. His hands were wide wide apart too, like my arse was four feet broad.

Everyone howled laughing. Chrissie laughed more than anyone.

He saw he was caught. He laughed. He said,

—Here Lisa, do you take it up the arse? I'd say you do—

I had my schoolbag in my hand and I swung it at him, hard, and I hit him on the face. Hard. A buckle must've caught him, cos there was blood. There was loads of blood.

Served him fucking right—

But it was assembly. Like the worst place ever for an Unprovoked Assault, in front of the whole school and all the teachers too. Teachers swarmed us, right away. They swooped in and bustled Simon off. They bustled me to the head teacher before I'd got my breath back.

I wouldn't say why. I wouldn't say to Sean either when he came to pick me up, I wouldn't say anything to him. I went to my room.

I rang Rocky. He didn't answer.

18.

He rang me on Friday. A few hours before I'd see him, the day before we were leaving.

—Hi! I said, all excited cos he'd be calling to make the final plans.

He didn't say anything at first. Then he did a big sigh. And he said,

—The money's away, babe—

It was like that echo again, my voice saying —What? like from miles away.

—I had to give it to Raymie, for his half of the car—

He was taking the piss, he had to be taking the fucking piss—

—You said tomorrow! I said. —You said—

My voice went high, nearly squeaking. There was a long pause and I knew I'd pissed him off.

—*You said, you said*! he snapped. —I know what I said! But the car's half Raymie's, he's hardly going to just give it to us—

I'll shag Raymie for it, I nearly said. But that was out, cos half the car was worth a hundred quid, and Raymie'd already shagged me for free so there was no way he'd pay a hundred for it—

Red spots came in front of my eyes. Rocky couldn't change his mind. He couldn't. I couldn't go back to school. Simon and his mates might trap me in the bogs like Chrissie and Petesy and Darren did. They might make me shag them. I'd thought that before, even before I hit him. It was something in his eyes when he looked at me, like he was thinking about it. Like could he get away with it. It was maybe why I'd walloped him, that look in his eyes.

I don't know how long the pause was this time. Then Rocky said,

—Do you still want to get away?

My heart jumped.

—Yeah, I said. —How?

Then I knew how.

—Can you meet me? I said. —At the end of the road here, now, so we can sort it out?

He sighed, all tragic. But he said, —Yeah. All right.

I ran round the corner to the car. I got in. Rocky gave me a tight little smile. Was he going to kiss me?

No.

—So, we're a bit fucked aren't we, he said. —What do you reckon we should do?

Right. I'd say it.

—We could get someone round again. Tonight. So we can still leave tomorrow—

I didn't want to. But even twenty or thirty quid would be OK now, just to put petrol in the car—

—OK, he said.

And my heart leapt.

—Just not— I said.

He laughed. Not a proper laugh, not a warm funny one. He rolled his eyes.

—I know, I know, only one fella—

I said nothing.

—You know if it's one fella we'll only be going away with twenty quid?

He saw I did and I didn't care. He did that sigh again.

—I'll see if that deal comes off today too, he said. —The one I was telling you about, I might get fifty or sixty quid for. The fella put it back to next week but I might be able to change his mind—

—Cheers, I said, loving him again and feeling bad for thinking he was being a dick.

I said, —Sorry, cos of making him push this fella to sort the deal tonight. But we were going! One fella tonight for petrol money, and we were gone. I loved him for that.

—Eight tonight at the flat, yeah? We'll get you home by twelve and I'll pick you up tomorrow morning—

I wanted to do that hugging myself thing again.

—Yeah, I said.

He kissed me on the cheek. His stubble scraped my face.

—See you later, he said.

19.

It gets bad now, worse. I'm leaving things out cos I can't say it all. But it's still remembering, it's still bad.

I'm pissed, writing this.

I'm writing it down. I'm writing it all down.

It can come out like a black tooth.

20.

I was in the shoes again, killing my feet, and the bra digging into me and the thong up my hole. I met Rocky at the door of his block.

And I followed him in.

I dawdled in the hallway a bit, cos I didn't know what type of fella would be waiting. So I didn't see Rocky lock the doo of the flat. I didn't even know he locked it til later. He never did any other time, so I didn't think.

But if I'd seen him, would I have said anything? Wouldn't I have told myself it was only so no-one would walk in?

I was thick. Thick as shit.

I can still see myself. Like in a film. Dawdling in the hall before my life changed.

And I want to hug me. For the shy brave smile I do, tottering in those shoes. I want to tell me to run, to get out. I want to tell me to run from Rocky and never see him again.

And I want to hit me too, cos I was such a thick bitch, and my ma and Paul were right.

It's like being punched in the stomach, remembering it now. How fucking obvious it all is. I should've seen it coming a mile away. I should've seen it when Rocky snogged me and said I was gorgeous.

Rocky put his hand at my back and steered me into the living room.

And it was full of men. Full.

I blinked, twice. Was I seeing stuff wrong, cos the only light was candles?

But the room was full of men.

OK, so Rocky was having a party and I'd take one man only one OK maybe two into the bedroom and that'd be it—

Rocky smiled. It was like the laugh earlier, not proper or warm. I flashbacked the man from last week, his demented eyes an inch from mine.

Rocky said,

—Lie down, Lisa—

My head sort of exploded. It's the only way I can describe it. Like getting punched and seeing stars and hearing a bursting noise inside your skull.

The pieces fell into place so fast I nearly heard them, like floor tiles dropping to boards. I knew what was going on. Why I was here. What was going to happen. I felt it in the air, crackling and maleness and danger.

This was it. This was how it would happen.

I didn't run. I didn't know then Rocky had locked the door, but I'd have no chance bolting for the door in these shoes.

And there were too many men.

Rocky spoke again.

—Lie down, Lisa.

I tried to say no, but my throat wouldn't work and did I think it was sand in my mouth the week before? This was more, this was a beach.

He was at me. He hauled my jumper over my head, rough and hurting my neck.

He pushed me to the floor. I fell, it hurt my elbow.

He pulled off my jeans. He ripped off the lacy thong, a new one tonight cos the one last week was ripped off me too. He yanked at my bra and it tore.

He was bigger than me. When I stopped fighting he shagged me. Right there on the floor in front of everyone.

Someone else. Pushing between my legs, a weight gasping out my breath. Tearing inside me.

He dug his nails into my tit. He came on my face.

(—Whoah, Rocky said, jumping back.)

Someone else. The third from last week, with the mad eyes. Maybe three's his lucky number ha ha three is a magic number—

Again he made me look. And that's how I saw someone taking a photo.

Someone else. —Givvis a big smile for the camera—

Someone else. He liked that I was crying. He dug into my throat.

My head screamed inside. Like that rush of feeling when you nearly walk in front of a car, only for ages and hours and ages and I couldn't breathe I'd die or maybe that's why I'm here they'll kill me they've paid Rocky so they can kill me—

More photos.

Someone else. Tommy, from the gulag.

—All right? he said to Rocky, and Rocky said back, —Go for it, mate.

It was worse it was him, someone I knew. Someone I sat with at dinner. It was worse. He could see my tits, he could see all of me—

He kissed me. Not a kiss to be nice, but like smothering me, and that was the worst of all.

21.

It was over.

Maybe. No-one was at me any more. They laughed instead, chuckling, like when you're in the best mood ever, it's your birthday or you've found a tenner on the street. Beer tins cracked open.

I lay there like a butterfly stabbed to a board. Could I sit up? If I tried they'd see and it might piss them off. Maybe they'd start all over again. They'd say, here no-one said you could go anywhere—

—Here, Rocky! Where's your bog?

—There—

More laughing. Rocky meant me, I was the bog, I knew cos of the flavour of the laughs. I could sit up, cos I did. They couldn't do that, I'd die—

—Calm down, Lisa, no-one's going to piss on you, for fuck's sake, Rocky said. His voice was bored.

More laughing. One of them started towards me. I think it was the *givvis a smile* one but everything was blurred in my head, the faces and hurt all together.

He leaned over me. I flinched like a dog about to be kicked. More laughing.

He grabbed my face.

—I'm not going to piss on you, love, calm the fuck down, he said.

He went to kiss me.

He shoved me away instead, back onto the floor.

Rocky laughed louder than anyone.

They went.

It was ages til they went and I lay on the floor, like an animal but happy ignored as long as they didn't start on me again. There was laughing and beer and handshaking and loads of calling each other mate.

But they went.

And it was me and Rocky left.

I lost it. When the front door closed I cried and howled like I'd never stop.

I yanked off the stupid fucking shoes and I grabbed my jeans and jumper and tried to pull them on, but my hands were shaking too much to button the jeans up, and the jumper was ripped round the neck. I put it on anyway and pulled the jeans up to my hips. Even that hurt. Even my skin hurt. I hurt all over. Between my legs and my chest where they bore down and my tits where they dug their fingers in and my throat where the last one choked me. And my back from being on the floor and my face from the third fella holding it. It hurt. It hurt.

—Fuck's sake, Rocky said, in that bored voice again, like I was the biggest fucking drama queen in the history of the universe. But I couldn't stop. I couldn't have stopped even with a gun to my head. My head pounded and I cried and snattered, but I couldn't stop.

—Look, he said. —If I'd told you before, you wouldn't have agreed, would you? And then we'd be fucked, one fella a week and months to get the money? We can go now, it's OK, we've got the money and we can go now—

But then why did he make me think that fella would piss on me? And Rocky held me down for the first one, and he laughed nearly louder than them all put together—

I didn't have the words. So I shook my head.

—Fuck's SAKE, he said.

He said,

—You can fuck off back to the home if you're going to get on like that about it. I was doing it for us, and I had to kind of play along with them, they paid more to have it a bit rough—

But he didn't tell me that—

I might've done it, if that'd been it. I might've, cos Rocky wanted it.

But he didn't ask!

Panic gushed in me about the gulag. I wanted to run out of that flat and never come back, but then what?

And this was me being a stupid bitch again, stupid bitch numero deux. Cos I thought, if I run out I won't get the money.

And it was my money. I'd fucking earned it, no-one could say I hadn't.

—Look, he said.

His voice was gentler now.

—I should've let you know first, OK. But I thought you'd say no, and I know you're dying to get away tomorrow. You can't stay in that home with them cunts—

What I said was so small even I couldn't hear it. He leaned in. I said it again.

—What about him who took the photos? It'll go round the place and everyone'll laugh at me—

This was nearly the worst thing. I'd saw the man holding the camera, his grin hazy on the outside of my eyes. He'd show the photos to Rocky, and Rocky would show them to Jim, and Jim would show them to Chrissie, and Petesy and Darren and Simon and everyone at school would see them and they'd laugh at me—

—It'll not, he said. —It won't, I promise, no-one's going to see them. That fella, he was just acting the hard man. I'll tell him to burn the negatives, even before he gets them developed—

—How?

He laughed.

—I've got dirt on him, he said. —Trust me, if I tell him to burn them he'll burn them. And I'll tell him, I swear I will—

Even more than the hurt, people seeing those photos was worse. Chrissie. The staff at the home. Everyone at school.

And that's when I decided. No-one would see those photos, whatever the fuck I had to do to stop it.

And so I believed him.

—OK, I said. It came out shaky but I said it. —OK.

—Right, he said. —And look, we've a hundred and fifty quid now so we can leave first thing in the morning. And we've got the car so we can get miles away before anyone even knows—

So I said OK, again.

THREE

Flat
———

'There isn't a town, village or hamlet in which children are not being sexually exploited.'

Police officer quoted by Sue Berelowitz, Deputy Children's Commissioner, in evidence to a House of Commons select committee, London, 2012

One young person who participated in a research interview still sometimes questioned whether she was to blame somehow, a few years on, even though the circumstances of her case clearly reveal this not to have been the case: 'I kinda think it was my fault, it was stupid me even saying hello to him'.

'Not a world away': The sexual exploitation of children and young people in Northern Ireland, Barnardo's Northern Ireland, 2011

———

1.

I forgot about the cameras I forgot about the cameras I forgot about the cameras.

I'm caught. Fucked. I was a stupid bitch at fourteen and I'm a stupid bitch now.

I knew there were cameras, course I did. It's the first thing Karen said about, years ago when I was in the squat with Nicola and Karen was showing us how to nick stuff from shops. So I knew about the cameras in the Spar the minute I walked in for my first shift. Two at the back. One over the milk fridge. One at the bread shelves. One at the front, pointing at the magazines.

But I never thought there'd be one at the till. I didn't even look. The cameras were for the shop, not for staff, I'd never have thought in my puff they'd be spying on the staff—

Niall's cashing up, he's took the till drawer to the tiny office at the back where the safe is. I lock the shop door and scoop up my pile of change from under the till. I take it home every day in case someone sees it and says what's this money here. I've got fifteen quid in my pocket today, so that's a hundred and forty five in total, hidden in my room in the hostel.

It's the twelfth of January.

Niall shouts my name.

His voice is wound up, urgent, so I think fucking hell has something fell on his head. So I nearly break my neck rushing out from behind the counter and through the shop to the office.

He's at the rickety table he counts the money at. Coins and bags and notes are all over the place but I hardly see them, cos I'm looking at Niall's face all red. Then I see the cupboard.

There's a screen's in the cupboard. I saw the cupboard ages ago, I think I did, but I never really noticed it. It's always locked and I don't think I even thought about it ever.

But it's open now. There's a screen in it.

I know what the grainy grey of the screen is right away, course I do. It's CCTV. And I look back at Niall's face and I know right away what's happened and that I'm totally, totally fucked.

—You've been taking money, Niall says.

And I can't say what the fuck, cos there on the screen like a scene from Crimewatch is me.

I'm looking up, on the screen, towards the back of the shop, and I'm putting my hand in my pocket. It's totally obvious I'm up to something, you could tell a million miles away from the way my face is.

I try anyway.

—I was putting something in my pocket, I say.

Then,

—I was getting a tissue.

His face goes even more bug-eyed. His mouth tries to say words.

—You've been taking money, he says again.

I've got like a second to decide. Less. I can say no I haven't. But I can see from his face that's not going to work.

I'm getting cold and hot all at once. All these thoughts whizz through my head, like a big flash. I think, I'll get angry and how dare he and I've never been so insulted in all my life and I was just getting a tissue out of my pocket. But he only has to find a different part of the tape, where I'm doing it again.

Or I can say yeah. Yeah, I did it. I can cry, make him do that concerned face again. He might even help me, cos it's no skin off his nose if the Spar loses a bit of money—

He said before if there was anything he could do. This is anything he can do.

So I let my face crumple.

—I had to, I say.

I cry. If I was acting I'd deserve an Oscar, but I'm not even acting. There's just the hostel, for years and years in front of me.

Niall doesn't say anything. He just looks at me.

I babble. It was only that one time, it was only a tenner, I was broke and I'd no money for food. I'm on the dole, I've no money.

He watches me. For a second I think he'll say OK.

But he doesn't.

—Please, Niall, I say. —Just delete the recording and no-one'll know and I'll never do it again—

He watches me.

I know what I can do. I know what'll work.

I move towards him. I grab at his zip.

He jumps back and gawps at me, like I'm trying to rape him.

And I have anger now.

It rushes the edge of my vision, a black scallop shape like it always does when I lose it. Niall's the one who needs a fucking Oscar, cos he's acting like I've murdered his firstborn. He can't be that fucking shocked. He's letting on to be, cos it's a fight he'll probably win and he never wins any. He'll like it.

He's just like everyone else. I thought someone was on my side but of course they're not.

—Do you think I'm stupid? he says. —I've gone back through these for the past two weeks—

I'm fucked.

I whisper that no-one has to know I'll never do it again please Niall.

—How much? he says.

I say forty. I swear. I needed it, I had no money.

—Please, Niall, I say again.

He says,

—I could call the police.

So then I lose it full time.

I go fucking mental. I scream at him. I don't really remember what I said cos it's been years since I lost it like that. But I know I said he's like everyone else, he said he'd help me and now he'll call the peelers. He hasn't a fucking clue, he lets on to be nice but he hasn't a clue, Mummy and Daddy pay his rent and he doesn't know a fucking thing about the real world—

That hits him where it hurts. His face flickers with it. It feels fucking amazing. There's roaring in my ears and I'm about to hit him.

—Get out, he says. —Get out and don't come back—

I grab my coat. It's on the peg above his head and as I slam my arm up for it he flinches.

I think about hitting him. I could beat the shit out of him, I know I could. But I still need him on side.

I say,

—Are you going to call the police?

We stand there, me panting. We're probably looking like people who've had a normal row, a Lover's Tiff. The question stretches out.

He thinks about it. He drags it out.

—No, he says at last.

And I don't wait for any more. I throw my coat on and slam myself out of the shop. I bang the door behind me, for the last time.

2.

It's only after my heart stops pounding and I've stormed my way to the city centre that I catch on what this means. If I'm sacked from the Spar the dole will cut me off. I'll be taken off benefits, all benefits. It's six months with no money if you leave or lose a work placement they find for you.

And if I've no dole, I've no Housing Benefit.

And if I've no Housing Benefit, I can't stay in the hostel. They said that the first day I got there. If you're not on any benefits we can't have you. Cos it costs them two hundred quid a week per resident to have us stay. And if the Housing Executive don't pay that, the hostel can't cover it.

So, I'll have to leave. Then I'll have no address for the Housing Executive to send me letters. I'll have to start on the list all over again in six months when I get the dole again and have an address to start with. I'll have to wait another three years for a place. And where will I live if they stop my Housing Benefit? I won't even have an address to apply for jobs.

I'm on a bench outside City Hall and I'm bawling like a kid. I don't care who sees me, I can't help it. This is why people jump.

I might jump. It's too much to sort out and I might jump.

3.

I don't remember much about getting home from Rocky's flat that night.

I stumbled on and on in the dark, like those nightmares in a fog when you're being chased. I cried. My head was too full. It wouldn't stop remembering, even after Rocky calmed me down.

I hadn't knew. That was it, I hadn't knew when it started that he'd arranged it to be rough. I'd thought it was real, it'd felt real—

I think I remember my feet hurting in the shoes, but everything else hurt too so I'm not sure. Even my ears hurt from when my tears had run down into them. And all I could hear in my head was that song, *three is a magic number oh oh three is a magic number*. It went round and round in my head, faster and faster, til I thought I didn't care what had happened and being sore, I'd go mad if it didn't stop. Like actually, really mad. If I could have torn my head off to stop it I would have.

I came home without my shoes. By the time I got home I didn't remember where they were. I think I left Rocky's house with them on but I think I might've threw them into a bush. There were cuts on my feet when I got back.

The staff buzzed me in and I saw the big wooden clock in the entrance hall. And it wasn't even eleven, and I remember blinking in the light of the hall not knowing why everyone was still up, cos it felt like years had passed.

I think the staff asked where were my shoes, and I think Chrissie laughed at me from the living room, but I don't know. I conked out nearly cold when I got to my room. It was like being pissed, I fell straight onto the bed and conked out.

And when I woke up the next morning it was like being pissed too, cos I couldn't remember getting home. I had a flashback, about hiding round the corner from Rocky's flat scared to walk home, and the wall I huddled against was cold on my arm. And my hand swinging up and the shoes sailing through the air in slow motion, tumbling against the dark. But I could have dreamt it. I didn't know.

It was only half seven but I got up, cos I should go early. And maybe he'd be already there. He'd said early. The earlier we went the more time we had before anyone noticed—

I had a shower. I stayed in for ages, far longer than when Chrissie had got Petesy and Darren to do that. I washed my hair. It was full of tangles and my scalp hurt. A lot of it came out when I combed it.

I sat on the shower floor with the water running. I wanted to be not me. There was no way out. There was nothing I could do. Cos even if me and Chrissie became mates again and people at school stopped picking on me, I was still in that gulag and I was still me.

And what had happened would always have happened.

I shaved my legs and under my arms. And I sank down and sat again on the shower floor, and I looked at the razor for a long time.

. . .

4.

He was there.

He didn't see me when I came round the corner, cos he was texting. I stopped for a second, stood at the corner holding my carrier bag with my toothbrush and a spare pair of knickers and my makeup and deodorant and my phone. I watched him, looking at him when he didn't know I was. Did I believe him about the night before, that it was for us? Maybe. Probably. And the photos?

And he looked up and saw me and he smiled, that expression for a minisecond when you see someone and can't hide how you feel. He was glad to see me. He meant it.

I went towards the car. I got in.

I got into his car.

But it was Belfast he drove us to. Belfast! What was the point of that, it was only like half an hour from the gulag. And how could we sleep in the car if we were in Belfast – park outside someone's house?

I thought maybe he'd maybe drive on into the countryside, or even to Larne to get the ferry to Stranraer and we could get to Scotland or England where no-one would ever find us. I didn't know if we had enough money for the ferry, but it couldn't cost that much—

But he didn't. He texted someone a couple of times along the way and I thought it might be Plans, but he didn't say anything so it mustn't have been.

We stopped on a ratty looking street, houses with crumbled paint and beer cans lying about and curtains still pulled in most of the windows.

—Why've we stopped here? I said.

And why are we in Belfast anyway, I wanted to ask, a smelly street in Belfast is hardly running away romantically into the sunset—

He pointed.

—See that B&B sign? My mate owns it. And he says we can doss here for a night, get our heads together and figure out our plan—

We didn't need a plan, I thought, apart from drive miles so no-one could find us. But this was good, this was better than sleeping in the car. And right like that I was knackered, like I could fall asleep right there in my seat. So I got out and I followed Rocky up to the door.

He banged the door for ages before anyone came to it. A girl opened it, a Chinese girl who looked about twelve.

—She's the cleaner, she lives here, Rocky said when she went to get this mate of his. I thought then maybe, sometime later, I could find a B&B for us both to live in, and I could clean it, and we could have money and a place to stay and things might be all right. Maybe I'd speak to her later, I thought, ask her how she got the job.

We stood on the doorstep. The door opened again. There was a man there, maybe about fifty, wearing tracksuit bottoms nearly falling down under his belly, and a stained red football top. He was wearing a wig so bad it looked like a hat

—All right, Michael? he said to Rocky. And that was funny cos I'd never even thought Rocky's name obviously couldn't be Rocky. I mean funny haha not funny weird, cos loads of people had nicknames and Rocky having one was no big deal. His real name had just never come up.

The man looked at me.

—Is it still all right about the room, Rocky said, and the man said aye, and we went up narrow stairs and along a creaky corridor and we were in a room and he gave Rocky a key and he left.

The room was ancient looking, with chipped furniture and a thin bumpy bedspread and grubby white — grey — wallpaper with tiny pink and yellow flowers. There wasn't even a carpet, only a rug. But there was a bed so I didn't care.

—I have to go out, want to get your head down? Rocky said, and said yeah, cos thank fuck he didn't want a shag.

He pulled the curtains. I had my jacket and boots and jeans and bra off and was under the covers before he left the room, and I sank straight down and down into a deep sleep.

It was getting dark when I woke up. Rocky wasn't back. I don't think I could've moved even if the room caught fire. It's like there was a weight on me. And a raw burning still between my legs. My chest still hurt too.

I went to sleep again.

When the door opened again it was full dark. It was Rocky and he'd brought KFC. The crispy hot smell drifted to me before I even saw the bag, and I got such a fast wave of hunger I was nearly sick. I hadn't eaten anything since dinner the day before.

He tossed the KFC bag onto the bed.

—That's yours, he said. —I've already had some. And I got some vodka for us as well for after—

I nearly loved him again. I could stay with him no problem if it was like this, a proper room together and KFC every night—

He pulled off his clothes, even his boxers. He got into bed. I had the KFC. He opened the vodka. We snuggled up under the covers, passing the vodka back and forth.

When I got tired again he held me. I fell asleep in his arms.

5.

On the Sunday it happened.

where is my cider

6.

The curtains in the room were like tissue so I woke up the next morning when it got light. It was maybe about six. Rocky was still sleeping. He lay on his back, snoring.

I was dying for a piss but I didn't want to wake him. I watched him, lying there. His mouth was open as he snored. His pubes were a dark smudge under a patch of sheet.

It was real now. This guy, sleeping beside me. This man. I'd never slept all night in the same bed as a fella. I could smell him in the room, grown and male. It made me feel good, adult. But a bit *what the fuck* too. I didn't know why.

I couldn't hold it any more, I had to go for a piss. I slid out of the bed. I pulled my jeans on under the T-shirt I'd slept in. I opened the door.

I didn't know where the bogs were so I stole out of the room and sneaked down the corridor, scared to open any doors in case they were rooms. I found a bathroom at the end of the hall. There was no-one about cos it was so early and the place was still dead, and for some reason I thought, I could go now if I'd put my boots and socks and bra on as well as my jeans.

It makes me cry and rage even now. I could've got away. I could've opened the front door and gone out into the whole world.

But I went back upstairs.

I creaked open the bedroom door and crept inside.

He was awake.

He was lying the same way but his eyes were wide open.

—Where'd you go? he said, and I said, —Bog, and he said, —C'mere.

I stepped over to the bed.

I was wary, I thought maybe he was looking a shag and I was still so sore. I could have done with never shagging another fella for the rest of my life.

I still feel like that.

He said,

—Take them clothes off and get in here with me—

Not rough, but kind of wheedling. Like he knew I didn't want to.

—C'mon, he said. —Or do you not want to any more, with me? Is that it?

—No! I said.

Now he'd think I was a bitch. Like I was someone like Chrissie, who played games with fellas just because.

—Well c'mon then, he said.

It took everything I had to say it, cos I was saying no and not being like the girls in the pornos taking it good any time. And what would he say if I said no? Maybe he'd kick me out. Dump me and leave me on my own.

But I couldn't, I couldn't. I was so sore.

I whispered

—It's a bit sore, I'm sore—

—Ach, he said.

I felt useless then.

—Sorry, I said.

He made his face like it didn't matter. But I could see it did.

He said,

—It's all right, just I'm horny cos of sleeping in the same bed with you. My balls are like watermelons—

I'd have to do it. I knew that fellas had to when they were really turned on, cos it was sore for them otherwise. Chrissie told me but everyone knew that anyway. So I was about to say OK, cos I'd have to manage. But he said,

—You turn me on so much, that's all. How about a blowjob?

So I did.

I thought maybe we'd get something to eat after, cos it was a B&B we were staying in and that was Bed and Breakfast, but after the blowjob Rocky went back to sleep. And when he woke up he looked at his phone and he said it was after eleven.

—C'mon, we'll hit the road, he said. So I got my carrier bag and we left the room,

The man who owned the B&B came into the hall. His wig was still on top of his head like a hat, I could see his grey hair under its brown.

He shook Rocky's hand. —Sorted? he said, and Rocky said aye.

The man didn't even look at me. I didn't care. I thought he was a creep. Wiggy old wanker, I said in my head when the door closed behind us. Wiggy old wanker.

I was feeling better now cos Rocky had been so nice, so I asked him where we were going.

—What's the plan? I said, keeping my voice lighthearted so he didn't think I was having a go. And as long as I wasn't back in the gulag I didn't care where we went.

He had a think.

I waited.

—How about we go to Bangor? he said. —We may as well, we're in no rush. We can take a walk on the beach.

I'd never been on a beach in my life, but I wasn't going to say it cos it would've sounded pathetic. And there was no way he was getting my thunder thighs into a bikini or even a swimsuit. But the beach sounded brilliant. I laughed.

—Yeah! I said.

That was my last day.

I wonder now did he give me a nice day on purpose, to be kind.

But I think now he was waiting for something, maybe for someone to get back to him or details to be sorted. He kept checking his phone and texting, and it kept buzzing with texts coming in. That's why nothing happened that first night. I think now he was keeping me on side.

We went shopping first when we got to Bangor. We went into charity shops and he bought me a pair of jeans, and a top that was maybe skimpy but maybe I thought I liked. We went into Boots as well and he got me some makeup and some body spray and a packet of lady shaver razors.

Then we went to the beach. I didn't have to worry about taking any of my clothes off, cos it wasn't warm enough. So we walked along the sand and we talked.

He told me more stuff about his dad, how his dad always hit him until Rocky was big enough to hit back. I nearly said then about Petesy and Darren wanking over me in the school toilets, but I didn't cos it was still too much to share. So I made nice noises instead, and then he stopped talking and looked out over the water. I felt really sorry for him.

He said, —Wait here for a bit, would you?

And he went down the beach, and up the steps, and round a corner and left me on my own.

I stood there for a minute. I thought, I'd better wait for him. But I thought, he's not going to come back. He's taken me to Bangor cos he knew I wouldn't know where to go from there. He's left me on my own.

I cried a bit.

7.

I talked to Gemma about it, a couple of weeks ago. I didn't tell her everything, but I said about being left on the beach and how I knew he'd gone.

And she said that me thinking right away he wouldn't come back, that was cos I was Obviously Depressed at that time. And that when you're depressed everything seems negative, but that's the depression talking.

But that's fucking shit I thought then, and I do now. I probably was depressed yeah, cos I can't remember a time when I haven't been, but being depressed isn't about life being rosy but somehow you think it's shit. Sometimes it's that your life actually is shit and you know it and the thought of being you for the rest of it is too much.

—How would you like to have been fourteen and left on your own on a beach somewhere, that wasn't the depression talking was it? I said to her.

And she didn't have an answer.

8.

It was two hours and thirty seven minutes before he came back. I sat on the sand against a wall, looking at my phone, wanting to text him but knowing I wouldn't. I cried a bit again. I counted to a hundred, loads, and thought every time if he didn't come back by then I'd go. The stuff I'd brought from the gulag was still in the car, but I had the bag with the charity shop clothes and the makeup in it. I'd go.

I counted to a hundred again. And again. And then he was there, strolling across the sand. He wasn't in a hurry.

I wiped my eyes fast. He came up. He had a carrier bag, it looked like there was a bottle in it.

—What's wrong with you? he said. —Have you been crying?

—No—

I could smell drink off him. He must've been in the pub.

I couldn't help it. I said,

—Where were you, you were away ages—

—Went to get us this, he said, holding up the bag.

—But you were away ages!

—I know, he said, —but I ran into a mate up the town and I hadn't seen him for ages and he made me go for a pint—

I cried a bit. I was scundered but I couldn't help it.

And he said, —Ach, love.

His voice was kind. He came over close and he put his arms around me.

—Ach, I didn't notice the time, he said. —I'm sorry, all right?

I told him it was all right, and it was. He was back now. But he still held me, laughing but not in a bad way, and he said, —So are we cracking open this bottle or what?

We opened the bottle and sat on the sand and he rolled a spliff. It was getting cold so I started wondering where we were sleeping that night, and after I had some spliff and vodka I had the balls to ask him.

—Sure we can sort it out later, he said.

Maybe we'd end up sleeping in the car, I thought. But I didn't really mind. It'd be my second night away from the gulag. I thought about them, wondering what they'd done when I hadn't come back. They probably thought I was in Rocky's and I'd come back later and if I didn't they'd send the peelers round. They mightn't even have bothered doing anything about it yet—

It was getting dark and I was getting cold now. I hoped he'd make up his mind soon about where we were going.

His phone beeped with a text.

—Do you want to head back to the B&B tonight? he said. —That was Billy, he's asking if we're sorted yet. He says if we're not and if we're still near Belfast we can have the room for another night. He says there's no-one there this week at all—

—All right, I said, cos I wanted to get into the warm, and even with Wiggy Wanker there a proper bed was far better than the car.

And tomorrow was another day. I'd heard that in a film somewhere. We'd be on the road properly tomorrow. I'd make him.

He lit a spliff in the car, one he'd rolled on the beach. It was strong, so I sucked hard on it and I necked vodka. So I was feeling nice and toasted when we got back to the B&B. I nearly thought I'd say hi to Wiggy Wanker.

The door was half open when we got there. Wiggy Wanker wasn't around, he was maybe off somewhere having a wiggy wank.

We went up to the same room as before and when Rocky pushed open the door I thought, here no harm, but I'd sack that wee Chinese girl if I was Wiggy Wanker, cos if she's the cleaner she's not doing much cleaning—

The bed hadn't been made, and the KFC bag and napkins were still on the floor. The empty vodka bottle was on the bedside table where we'd left it. We hadn't had an ashtray so we'd used an empty cigarette box and that was still there on the table at the side of the bed, overflowing and stinking. The whole room was stinking. No-one had even opened the window.

But it was a bed, and no-one knew I was there. I sank down on the bed right away. I still felt like I could sleep for weeks.

Rocky smiled down at me.

—Do you fancy having a bath? he said. —I could head out and get us some food—

—Yeah, I said, laughing up at him, cos suddenly those two things, a warm bath and some warm food, sounded like the best things ever.

He laughed back.

He even ran the bath for me. And he found a big towel for me. Not a huge fluffy white one like you'd get in hotels, it was thin and beige and ratty, but still. He brought the bag from Boots too, with the razors and the makeup and the perfume.

—I'll be back in about half an hour, make yourself look nice, he said. He winked at me and laughed.

And I laughed back and said I would. I wouldn't say no to him tonight, I didn't care if I was sore.

9.

I always used to love baths. Apart from getting wasted and lying sprawled on the floor listening to music, I thought they were the most chilled thing you could do. Which is funny as they're hot, haha.

I wallowed. It's the only word for it. I could see my stomach, sticking out of the water like I was a hippo, but I tried not to think about it. The water was warm and I was half pissed and there was food on the way and bed and cuddles and spliffs. Even if there had to be a shag first. Who cared, it couldn't be that sore. And I wouldn't think about the other night. I wouldn't think about it again, so there.

I shaved my legs and under my arms and had a look at my fanny to check it was still OK after the wax. It was still smooth and bald. It looked weird, I looked like a kid. I couldn't see what fellas see in waxed fannies but what did I know.

I didn't want to get out of the bath, but Rocky had said he'd be half an hour and to make myself look nice. That was a sexy thing to say. And I was sexy too. Here I was in a B&B with my grownup boyfriend, about to stay the night with him. And every next night. And it was cos of me earning the money that we could do it. And I wouldn't think about that night again, ever.

I got out of the bath. I got dried. I sprayed perfume in front of me and walked into its cloud, the way I'd seen someone do on telly. I put on makeup. He'd got me foundation and blusher and lipstick, and the blusher and the lipstick were too red, hooker red, but I put them on anyway cos he'd picked them and he'd said to look nice.

I heard the door rattle in its lock. I laughed cos that was him back, impatient.

It must have been the red lipstick, cos I thought, I'll be a bit of a tart. I dropped my towel. I swayed my hips over to the door. I thumbed back the lock. I opened the door.

It was Wiggy Wanker.

The shock of it was like being punched in the face. I couldn't move. He wasn't Rocky. And I was in the nip, wearing the lipstick of a tart and a splayed slutty grin.

He grinned. He thought I was smiling at him on purpose! My head scrabbled. Shut the door no get the towel no shut the door shut the door—

I slammed at the door. I tried to slam it shut. He threw his arm up to block it. He blocked it. And then he was inside the room. He was inside the room inside the bathroom with me and I had no clothes on and what was he doing—

I tried to reach the towel, puddled on the floor beside the toilet. I swooped down for it. I got a grip on it. He ripped it out of my hand.

And I knew. Like the other night with the men I knew exactly what was going to happen. But this was even worse. There'd be no thinking after, well it might've been all right. That it might've been arranged for money for us to go away.

I leapt back so hard my arse hit the cold sink. But I couldn't go any further. He was still there. He was looking.

I tried to squeeze into myself. I crossed my arms over my tits and tried to squeeze my fanny in between my legs so he couldn't see. Even if Rocky burst in right now it was still terrible, cos this man had seen me in the nip—

But he reached out. He wrenched my arms apart. It took no effort, it was like I was a doll—

He hauled me to the floor.

After, he lifted his hand from my mouth and he pushed my hair back from where it'd fallen over my face. He did it gently, like he was my boyfriend, and like Tommy smothering me with a kiss in Rocky's flat, somehow that was the worst of all.

He got up. I scrabbled back on my arse, bumping against the stand of the sink. He looked at me. Staring like he was trying to imprint my face in his memory. He'd probably have a wank about it later, this fourteen year old girl naked on the floor crying. I was in his wank bank, like forever. I got such a big sob at that one I hurt my chest. Cos even though it was over I couldn't help what he did with it after. Who he told and the way they'd laugh at me and say it'll harden her. And I thought about that man with the camera, and it'll be in loads of wank banks too unless Rocky had told the fella to burn the negative and he had—

All this, from him pushing my hair back to me sobbing and thinking about wank banks, happened in about two seconds. My mind was going like a million miles an hour, going *wankbankwankbankwankbank*, and speeding up and getting louder so I thought my head would explode with it. Fuck off, I told Wiggy Wanker in my head, fuck off fuck off fuck off and leave me on my own—

Rocky was there.

I'd sort of curled into myself when I was sobbing, sitting near under the sink, and I didn't want to look up in case Wiggy Wanker was looking at me with that face. Like he'd pat me on the head and tell me I was a good girl.

But I had to keep an eye on him, cos who knew if he'd finished or what he'd do next, he might call the Chinese cleaner girl in for a threesome. So I looked up, fast so he wouldn't see me, and I saw Rocky's legs in the doorway.

—Rocky, I wanted to say, but I knew my voice wouldn't do it. But it must be obvious what had happened. And now Rocky had come back and now he'd kill Wiggy, he could stab him and I'd stab him too and we could run and get down to Dublin first then over to England—

Rocky's legs came into the room. Slowly, not like angry. Why was Rocky not cracking up, going mental? Even if he didn't know what'd happened, Wiggy was standing there over his girlfriend while she was crying in the nip?

The legs stopped beside me. I looked up. Rocky was looking at me, and like with Wiggy Wanker his eyes were bright.

It looked like he was trying not to laugh.

—C'mon, he said.

I didn't move cos I didn't get it. C'mon where? Were we leaving, and why wasn't he killing Wiggy and did he expect me to get up in front of Wiggy when I was still in the nip—

He reached down. He grabbed my arm.

—C'MON! he said and still I didn't get it, why was he pissed off? Was it cos I'd opened the door to Wiggy, was that it? Wiggy couldn't have got in if I hadn't unlocked the door, and Rocky must know that, so was it my fault—

Rocky pulled me up.

I was still crying, harder now, cos I was even more scared and I didn't know what was going on.

—Would you shut up! Rocky shouted, and he was trailing me down the hall and it hurt and what was going on?

The door of our room was open. The rubbish was away, piled in the KFC bag and put into the corridor. The Chinese girl must have cleaned it, or did Wiggy while I was in the bath? Cleaned the room to put me back into it after—

I fought then. I didn't know what was going on and why Rocky was pissed off, but there was no way I was staying in this B&B tonight if this Wiggy fella was here too—

Rocky threw me onto the bed.

He pinned me down.

He stuck his knee in my stomach.

He hit me.

10.

—Fucking wise up would you, he said. —You're not going nowhere—

He hit me again.

I stopped fighting, only cos he was hurting me and cos I had to tell him what had happened.

I didn't know why he was pissed off but he didn't know what'd happened.

—That man, I said. —Billy—

—What about him?

He sounded the lazy way he had after — the other night. Like he didn't want to hear it, like it was boring.

I said,

—He — made me. He had sex with me but he made me—

I couldn't say the word. I don't know why. I still can't, even in my head.

But he laughed.

He laughed!

He said,

—Why do you think you're here?

He stared at me.

He said,

—Did you think I wanted to run away with you, like we're in some fucking film or something? You're here to make money for me and that's the end of it—

I whispered no. At least I think I did, I couldn't hear me.

I froze, hot and choking on the bed.

I still wasn't sure, it was too big. It was because Rocky was pissed off at me maybe. Maybe I should have gone ahead with Wiggy Wanker, maybe Rocky had arranged it—

I felt sick come up. I was still in the nip and I felt like millions of people were watching. Like I was on a stage. I was prickling, like someone had rolled me in nettles. I tried to curl into myself again but I couldn't cover all of me, not with just my arms.

—And here, he said, leaning right into me so I could smell the drink on his breath, and I'd never felt so sober in my life.

—Cos of your *running away* stunt, no-one even knows where you are! Cheers for that, I couldn't have planned it better myself—

And that was it – I went for him. I was all tits and hair and nails and teeth, and I didn't even think for that second that I wasn't wearing anything.

But that, and him being bigger, and a fella, made me lose. You can't fight someone properly if you're not wearing anything either, you don't have your head in the right space.

I got a scratch on his face, I near got his eye, but everything was hot and loud and sore and I was twisted upside down and he'd banged my head off the wall.

I was sick, over and over til I felt like I'd die from it. It was coming down my nose, I was choking.

—For fuck's sake, he said. —What the fuck's wrong with you—

He opened the door. He shouted for Billy.

I went mad. I screamed he couldn't bring Billy in here, if he did I'd kill him, do you fucking hear me I'll fucking kill him.

Under the roaring in my ears I could hear someone coming down the corridor and I waited, gasping, because if it was Wiggy Wanker I'd kill him. Even if I had to do it by sticking my fingers into his eyeballs and even if Rocky killed me after.

I mean it even now, I would've killed him if I could have and I wouldn't have cared if Rocky killed me. I didn't want Rocky to win but at least I'd get killed knowing I'd killed Wiggy Wanker too.

It was the Chinese girl. Rocky didn't say anything to her, he just gestured at the sick on the floor and she nodded yes, yes, and scuttled away and came back with a mop and bucket. It was the most freaky, most weird thing ever, me curled into the corner in the nip, and Rocky on the end of the bed smoking, and this girl cleaning up around us.

She went away. Rocky finished his smoke.

He didn't offer me any or one for myself, and I copped on he'd no food either. I don't mean I was hungry, fuck's sake I didn't think I'd ever feel hungry or eat again for the rest of my puff, but that meant he'd been lying when he said he was getting food. He'd wanted to get me in the bath, so Wiggy Wanker could come up and maybe break in if I hadn't opened the door. Or maybe if I hadn't opened the door Wiggy would've got Rocky to call me to open it, they'd probably been sitting downstairs the whole time drinking vodka and planning it—

He stood up.

—Well, he said, chirpy like he was on a yacht or something, —laters—

And he opened the door and went out.

And he locked the door behind him.

11.

I'm in a bar. It's quick now I've decided, so I go straight to the bar and I wait. It's easy, what to do. I might be homeless tomorrow, once Niall tells his boss and the boss rings the dole. So I have to be quick.

I know what to do.

I checked my money and I had three fifty, enough for a drink. So now I'm in this bar. A rough one in the city centre I've heard about in the hostel. I've heard the fellas there saying things about this bar, so that's why I'm here.

I order the cheapest thing, a bottle of Becks for two quid, and I sit on a stool at the bar. I don't pick up the newspaper there or keep my eyes down shy. I stare around the pub. I make it obvious I'm waiting.

I look like shit, my hair's still pulled back for work and my eyes are tiny from crying.

But it doesn't take long. Maybe cos I look like I've been crying. Two fellas are at me within minutes.

They're taking the piss, passing the time. There's danger off them. I ignore them and they call me a frigid cunt and say here what's that burn mark on your face you freak. Then they fuck off.

The barman watches.

I sip the Becks.

Two more fellas, younger ones, about my age.

—Are you on your own?

I smile and say yeah.

—Called in for a quick one after work, I say.

And when we've done where do you work and where do you live and do you know such and such, I have another Becks, that the smaller fella buys me. Alan, he says his name is. The other one's Stevie.

We look, letting on not to. We eye each other up.

We play pool, still pretending this is all. Stevie buys me another Becks, then another. Then it's last orders. Kicking out time.

Someone has to say something. Alan does.

—Come back to ours for a drink, Chrissie? he says. —We're just round the corner—

Here's where it's tricky. This is new for me, saying it first. But I do.

—How much?

They're stunned.

They stop.

I could be dead here, cos if they say a price and I go back to their place – they can do what they want. They can say to the peelers I said OK. I'm in more danger than even back then, cos now I know.

And I'd never tell the peelers anyway, I'd never make a fucking peep. I've never done this before, not like this, but I know that much.

They called me a prostitute after the fire.

No fucking way I'll ever go to the peelers. Never, no matter what.

But it's all right, cos Alan and Stevie are kind. They're stunned but they say all right and we go back and I do it and they pay. I fuck them both but they're OK fellas. And now – I've got a hundred and ninety five.

12.

If I say *I cried* it sounds like crying a tiny bit. Weeping. Ladylike tears to dab with a tissue, and fanning my face like someone crying on Pop Idol, and then it'd be OK.

It wasn't like that. I shrieked so loud I was nearly sick again. I choked and gagged. I tried to stop so they couldn't hear. Rocky and Wiggy somewhere in this damp B&B, laughing at me.

I couldn't stop. Not for a long time.

Then the men began to come.

Over and over and over.

The first one ripped my top, cos I fought. He had BO, I was sick after. I did it in the carrier bag from the charity shop. I crouched on the floor. I couldn't breathe.

13.

I'm sacked.

I'm in bed when there's knocking on my door. It's bad news, I know right away.

I unlock the door. It's Gemma. I get back into bed and huddle the duvet around me. My eyes feel wild, staring.

—What happened at the shop, Lisa? she says.

I'm about to cry. I stare at the duvet, hard.

She says the dole's rung. My placement's over cos the staff caught me stealing from the till.

Fucking Niall.

—Were you? Gemma says.

I can't even say no, cos if I open my mouth I'll cry.

—Oh, Lisa, she says.

I know what's next. I don't want her to say it, cos then it's happening.

She says it.

—The dole says you'll probably be sanctioned—

She's worried, she says. She doesn't care about the dole, but it's the housing benefit. If my benefits are stopped I have to leave the hostel.

I know Gemma hates this, cos she said on Christmas Day when it was just her and me and Debbie. Kicking people when they're down, she called it. But the hostel manager has to have housing benefit for every day we're here and that's it. They're a charity and they can't pay it back if it gets stopped.

I'm paid up for rent til the end of the month, but that's only two weeks. I'll be homeless in two weeks.

Gemma says will I go down to the dole today and see what they say. She says she can't advise me to lie but maybe I could say it was a misunderstanding. And if I get sanctioned we can appeal. I say I will.

Up to thirteen weeks I could lose my money for.

My life is over.

14.

I started to go somewhere else. I made myself think about not being there. I couldn't at first. I didn't even know it was a thing. But I did it, and then all the time. Ages later, days and days or even weeks. I forget. I'm not counting.

I could sort of see myself from the ceiling. Like I was out of my body, watching it on a stained sheet with a man on top. The man had beige trousers, pushed down. He kept his shoes and socks on. When he moved his arse wobbled.

Sometimes I'd go right away, right through the ceiling and outside and over the houses like flying. They were my favourite ones. After lots of men it happened, first every couple of days and then most days. I could never make it happen every time.

I should say what happened after I got locked in, those first men.

But I can't write it all.

Here are some bits.

One man was posh. Like a teacher, about fifty. I thought about school, not the one me and Nicola were expelled from or the one with Chrissie, but a proper school, where people liked me. The teachers said I was doing well. I'd go places. I'd go to university.

Two of them couldn't speak English. They came in together. One watched and then the other.

I wanted to be a vet, when I was a little kid. So the teachers in my head said I'd go places and I did. To university and then I was a vet. I had a house of my own. I had a dog, a boxer like Molly from foster care with Mandy and Marty. Maybe I could've stayed with Mandy and Marty, they'd been all right. So I'd been let stay with them instead of having to go to the gulag, and I got my GCSEs and my A levels, and Mandy and Marty (and Molly) were at my university graduation. Molly wore a bow tie over her collar, a red one tied at the side. Mandy said she was really proud of me.

One man pretended to be kind. Maybe he thought he was being kind. That was worse, cos I was fourteen and crying, and if he was kind he would've left. He put his hand on my shoulder. He used my name. The way teachers and social workers do. Lisa Lisa are you all right Lisa. He called my name when he did it to me. Rocky and Wiggy Wanker would be laughing at that, down below.

One was a student. He put his books on the table beside the bed.

One smacked my arse, over and over til I screamed.

One was a peeler, still in uniform.

I floated.

14.

I only saw Rocky twice more. The door unlocked the morning after the first night and it was him.

I screamed right away. What the fuck are you doing, let me go, I'm going to fucking kill you—

He looked bored.

Wiggy Wanker was there too and they took me to the bathroom, the one where Wiggy had—

They said I had five minutes, and then they took me back to the room. But it was always Wiggy for the bathroom after that. Maybe Rocky couldn't be arsed with me. And when I next saw him, that's when I was moved.

I tried to get out, course I did.

I thought I'd fight Wiggy the next time they let me out to the bathroom, but I knew I hadn't a hope. So I'd have to escape. If I couldn't get out the door then I'd get out the window. It was a big drop, but I'd risk it if I was able to. Even if I broke my legs people would be in the street to help me.

I checked the window again the first night. It wouldn't open. It was painted shut and I tried so much I thought the vein in my neck would pop. It didn't work. Maybe I could unstick it with something sharp, but of course there was nothing.

And if I'd something sharp I would've stabbed Rocky. Stabbed him and took my chances with Wiggy Wanker afterwards.

I thought they might kill me.

That sounds calm, writing it like that, like *ho hum maybe they'll kill me*. But it wasn't when I felt it in my head. It was screaming panic, panic that I swallowed by then so Rocky or Wiggy didn't laugh at me or hit me. The first times I got the panic I couldn't help it and I screamed til it felt like my throat would bleed. Rocky had to let me out NOW, I'd fucking kill him, let me out NOW.

(Then I'd cry and beg and plead. I'd cry through the door please let me go please I won't tell anyone I swear. None of it worked.)

But mostly I thought about getting away.

15.

I cry and beg and plead and finally curse in the dole. But they don't care. They're going to stop my money for the full thirteen weeks.

—*Count yourself lucky you weren't arrested too,* the dole woman says. *She's like Niall, cos it's no skin off her nose but she knows she can have a go. She's acting like it was her shop and her money.*

—*Oh Lisa,* Gemma says again.

I'm crying now, I can't help it.

I'm going to jump.

I can't stay in the hostel with the phone calls back and forth between the staff and the dole and the Housing Executive. I have to get out. I can't just wait there to be homeless. I've maybe three, five days, a week, then I'm out. I hate Niall. I hate him nearly more than Rocky.

notthinkingaboutthattnotthinkingaboutthatnow—

I see Debbie on the stairs. We're sort of matey since Christmas Day – at least, we say hi.

She says hi now. She looks at me. I've been crying, it's obvious.

If she asks—

—*What's wrong?* she says.

I look at her. I decide.

We're in a flat. A mate of hers, Debbie says, but I know it's not. It's like every flat I've ever been in, except the apartment one that terrible summer. It's more of a squat.

We wait for the men.

It was piss easy to arrange, I knew it'd be.

—What's wrong? Debbie said, and I said, —I need money.

She knew what I meant. She said,

—I'm heading round to a mate's flat, if you fancy coming—

And I did.

I'm wearing jeans and my hoodie and a vest top. I don't dress up, I don't need stripper shoes. No-one will give a fuck about any of that, cos I'm not fourteen now.

We wait for the men.

16.

And then Chrissie was there. Like a fucking gulag reunion, haha.

I was still in the B&B, for weeks it felt like. Sun seeped through the curtains all day, then it got dark but the room was still stuffy and warm.

Men were there always. Early in the morning, in their work clothes. At night, and throughout, dawn and early morning pissed from drinking the night away. Old men in good jumpers one night more than any — Chrissie'd told me about them, men who dropped their wives in town for Thursday late night shopping first.

I couldn't sleep, cos my head was stuffed of cotton wool like being stoned. I shivered a lot too, maybe cos I wasn't eating. Wiggy brought sandwiches, ham and cheese ones from Tesco, but I didn't eat them. I drank the Coke he brought too, but sandwich bites were too big even chewed. I'd try, then spit. I'd get skinny, I thought. The Rocky diet, haha.

A key rattled in the door and it banged open. I looked up and it was Rocky. The second time I'd seen him since he'd locked me in here. The last time I'd ever see him, though I didn't know that then. (Unless I go for revenge. I think about that a lot.)

He came over. He pulled the covers off me.

—Get dressed, he said.

I thought maybe he'd let me go. How fucking stupid is that. So I didn't go for him, try to claw his eyes out. I dressed, in the jeans and the top ripped nearly in half. I couldn't see my boots, or my socks. They might've been in the room, but looking for them would be running a marathon.

Wiggy Wanker was in the hall, smirking. Two men were beside him. I didn't take in what they looked like except that one was small. The two of them and Rocky pulled me outside. Rocky put his hand over my mouth.

I really thought they'd kill me.

17.

There was a van. Small, no windows in the back, the type me and Nicola used to call paedo-mobiles. Rocky half shoved, half lifted me in, quick. I screamed and kicked. He slammed the door, so all I heard was me. Then seconds later, the van, roaring off fast.

I kicked the door so hard I had to stop before I broke my feet. Big deal if I did, but then I couldn't run. I scrabbled at the door so hard the blood was warm and wet on my fingertips. They'd kill me they'd kill me they'd kill me—

The van stopped. Feet crunched on gravel.

The door swung open.

I screamed, right away cos I couldn't help it. They'd kill me they'd kill me they'd kill me—

A man slapped his hand over my mouth. And then I was out of the van and in a building. Like a lobby, painted white and spotless and pot plants all around. A posh place. An apartment block maybe, like the ones in the city centre.

There were three flights of stairs, the men kept hold of me the whole way.

There was an apartment. A living room, painted white. A cream carpet. Heavy brown curtains, pulled, hanging to the floor. A brown leather couch and a TV on a cabinet. How a hotel room would look, maybe.

It was the cream carpet made me think they wouldn't kill me, cos it'd be too hard to clean up the blood. And why bring me here to kill me when they could do it in the van—

I started crying. I couldn't help it. I did big heaving sobs, standing on this thick cream carpet in my bare feet. The men ignored me, going round flicking switches and opening cupboards.

Then they both – well I know what, and how many times can I write it.

18.

After, I cried more, in the room they'd done it to me in. It had a double bed with a headboard and brown sheets like shiny chocolate. It was comfy, far better than the B&B. I've come up in the world, I thought, and I didn't stop crying for a long time. I did it quietly cos I could hear the TV in the front room and the men were still there.

I'll wait til morning, I thought, to see how to get out. There must be a window that opens. And if there's not I'll scream, soon as I'm alone. It's a block of flats, someone'll hear me—

I'd get out. But not back to the gulag, if anyone made me I'd run away. It was summer by then. I'd live in the woods, somewhere no-one could find me. I'd build a shelter somehow or maybe nick a tent.

I needed the bog. I didn't want to get up, in case the men were still there and they'd do it to me again. But they'd wake me anyway if they wanted. So I got up.

I looked for a nightie or a dressing gown. I felt stoned again, like this was a hotel. Course there was nothing. I put the jeans and the ripped top on. I'd still no shoes.

The bog was down the hall, past another bedroom like the one I'd left. The bathroom had black tiles and a big deep bath. This was like a flat I'd like when I was older, if I could be a vet. I cried more while having my piss.

There was no lock on the bathroom door, just a hole in the wood. No window, so no escape.

Back to the bedrooms. Only a tiny window in those, both way up and the size of a loaf.

—You'll not get out, a voice said.

I screamed.

I couldn't turn round. Caught, caught, I was caught, he'd kill me, beat me worse than Paul ever had—

—You hear me? the voice said, closer now.

A hand wrenched my shoulder and pulled me around.

It was the smaller man. His eyes stared right into mine. He had stubble and glasses. A nest of blackheads clustered around his nose. It was all I'd seen, earlier when he did it to me.

—C'mon into the living room, he said. —You and me are going to have a wee talk.

He said he'd kill me. A peep out of me or shouting or opening the curtains in the living room — that'd be it.

I was crying again. Course I was, I never fucking stopped.

I believed him.

He said the living room windows were painted shut like the B&B, but I already knew I wasn't going to try them. No-one knew where I was, he said. No-one would know if something happened—

He said, casual,

—Heard of the UVF?

I said nothing, cos course I had, who hasn't. He knew that. But he stared at me, intense, so I whispered yeah.

—Yeah, he said.

He pushed up his sleeve. He showed me the tattoo on his forearm.

—That's who you're dealing with, he said. —Remember that.

He meant they'd shoot me if I tried anything, or told anyone. I never forgot it. As I say, telling this now is only for me.

19.

Gemma comes up to my room again. It's where I am all the time now. She says she's been ringing and ringing the Housing Executive and she finally got through to someone who was all right and this person said I can declare myself to them as nil income. It might mean they consider a new claim, she says. She says one of the other staff will go down with me tomorrow. Maybe she can see I can't be bothered.

—What if they turn this claim down, I say, and she says she doesn't think they can, cos I have no income. But if they do then I can go to the Housing Executive's homeless unit and declare myself homeless again and ask for emergency accommodation in a B&B or another hostel, one that they have to pay for cos I'm homeless.

—What about my points, I say, —what about the housing list?

And she says I might have to start again.

I'm out of here.

But the next day I go down to the Housing Executive anyway, cos the staff corner me when I'm in the kitchen. Eleanor takes me. She's one of the snobby ones, I hate her. You shouldn't have been so stupid it's your own fault *is in the atmosphere of her car so thick I can nearly feel it.*

She takes me into the Housing Executive office like I'm a kid. I sign forms and that's a new claim made. They say I'll hear within the week. It's a week until the end of the month too. If the Housing Executive doesn't acept this claim then I have a week before I'm homeless.

20.

I was in the flat for weeks. Months. I sort of forgot anything else.

The Blackheads man was there a lot, every day. He brought men in but sometimes it was just him.

The other one was baldy, with piggy eyes and glasses. He made a noise when breathing, it was worse when shagging. I called him Wheezy in my head.

It never got better. I never got used to it. Most times it was so sore I cried during, and I nearly always cried after. And I'd still be sore then it'd be another man. Every time was like the first time. It never got better. It burned and it hurt and I cried.

Blackheads brought food every day. He brought smelly stuff as well, Alberto Balsam shampoo and Tesco Value shower gel. A razor, cos I'd to tidy myself up he said.

I lay in the bath looking at it. But he'd made me leave the door open. And he took the razor after.

I was eating. Not loads, but some, cos it hurt if I didn't. I had toast in the morning and another slice at night. I didn't bother with the ham paste there was, I just had Flora. There was no tea or coffee cos there was no kettle, maybe they thought I'd throw boiling water at them and I would've. Mostly I had water.

The jeans wouldn't stay up now but Blackheads bought other stuff, tiny skirts and sparkly slut tops I wouldn't be seen dead in. I felt like a doll dressed up in them, and that was scundering too.

I watched TV. Daytime TV. The Big Breakfast. This Morning. Bob the Builder. Local news, always. Maybe there'd be something about me, that I was missing. There never was. It makes me nearly laugh now, like there might've been.

Wish You Were Here. Who Wants to be a Millionaire. News. Jill Dando. Stormont. Late Night Poker. Eastenders and Coronation Street and The Bill and Casualty. Even Antiques Roadshow if nothing else was on. Old films and stupid films and kids' films and cartoons, I watched them all.

But I couldn't have said what happened after. I don't remember ever smiling at the funny bits.

A lot of the time I didn't finish watching them, cos a man would be there. I just got up, whoever it was. It was easier. And quicker. It'd hurt anyway, so why get walloped as well.

Some would do it while someone else watched. Then they'd swap. I waited for it to be over, to go back to TV.

We went out sometimes. Not to a club or pub. To parties. House parties, in posh houses mostly. Blackheads would text about the parties on his phone and when enough people said yes, he'd get me into the van.

One house had a pool, I had to lie down on the tiles beside it in front of everyone. That was the worst time maybe, but that's one I don't think about. There was a club once, about four in the morning, with the staff, off shift and coked up, twisting my nipples and laughing,

Mostly there'd be other girls at these parties, but sometimes it was just me. I'd be nearly in hysterics after. They let me drink sometimes, a lot, like near a whole bottle of vodka sometimes. But it only helped a bit.

Blackheads let me sit in the front of the van. I'd watch people in the streets, laughing in the orange glow of lights. Having lives.

I thought about jumping out, at traffic lights. I could run and by the time Blackheads pulled the van over and parked I'd be away—

I never did. It was too scary. He'd shoot me. And no-one knew where I was.

21.

And then Chrissie was there.

I could've hugged her right away, cos I hadn't talked for weeks and loneliness was bad too.

But she battered me round the head, over and over, so sometimes being alone is all right too.

I was in bed one night. I knew it was early July by then cos of all the Union Jacks and bunting all over the lampposts outside for the Twelfth, but I knew it wasn't the Twelfth yet cos there hadn't been the noise.

I was in bed one night and the front door opened and two men were talking and I wanted to cry.

One man was Blackheads. I tried to hear if the other one was Wheezy, but then there was a scream. A girl.

—Fuck off, fucking get off me!

I didn't know who it was. But I knew what they were doing to the girl, Blackheads and Wheezy.

And I lay clenched up under my covers in case they came in and got me next. I'd like to say I went in tough and kicked ass and rescued her, but course I didn't. I lay there curled up and hoped it wouldn't be me next.

It went quiet.

I heard the front door close and for a minute I thought they were all away, but I heard someone crying in the living room. It was big sobs, ones when you think the force of them will pull your heart out.

I should've went out but I didn't. Blackheads and Wheezy might come back and if they saw me up, it'd be my turn. That was stupid I knew, cos they'd have got me up if they wanted to, but I couldn't help it, I couldn't go in.

And part of me, well, I couldn't be bothered. I should feel like a real cunt about that but I didn't, not then. Not even now if I'm honest. I thought, I wish she'd shut up so I can go to sleep, and, that's nothing love, wait til you've been here a couple more weeks.

But it was Chrissie. Someone shouted my name and I woke up and she was there.

We stared like we'd never met before, Chrissie in the doorway and me in the bed.

She had on her Sugar Plum Fairy skirt, rumpled and dirty. And her white top and those stupid sparkly pink and white trainers, and how did she have shoes when I didn't?

—Chrissie, I said.

She came over, fast, in one movement.

She hit me.

—Are you going to tell me, she screamed, —what the fuck is going on?

She thought it was me, see. She thought me and Rocky and More-the-Merrier had planned it.

—No, I said, when my mouth was out of her hair and she was crying. —No—

It happened to her nearly the same way. She told me, her voice high and fast, sitting there in her dirty Sugar Plum Fairy skirt.

She said her and Jim had been seeing each other more and more, and she'd been telling the staff to fuck off when they Raised an Issue about it. She ran away to Jim's flat all the time, only going back for a change of clothes.

—The gulag staff rang the peelers about you, she said. — The peelers took your name down and what you looked like and that was it. No-one really said anything about you after that—

I nearly cried. I hadn't wanted anyone looking for me, not when I first left, but I didn't think they'd brush me over that fast.

Chrissie knew I was with Rocky, cos More-the-Merrier told her. Away in Dublin somewhere, maybe even over to London, he said, so she thought about it too, getting away.

He meant her to do that, I knew when she said. But I didn't say, in case she hadn't figured it out. I wouldn't put that look in her eyes, even if I didn't like her.

But he hadn't told her to shag men for money, and she hadn't had a threesome. He'd said he had a couple of hundred quid saved and did she want to go. She said course she fucking did and when could they leave?

—So he says, she said, —Well, when do you want to? So I says, Tomorrow, cos it's the school holidays so I can go whenever, you know? So he says tell the staff I was going to the shopping centre or into town or wherever, and to meet him at his flat—

That was three days ago. She thought.

She'd met him, makeup and hair straighteners and a change of clothes in a carrier bag. He drove them to Belfast, to the B&B. They spent the day in town, then when they went back he'd said he was going out to get food. (—KFC? I said, and she said, —No, pizza, looking at me like I was mental).

She'd had a bath. The door unlocked, a slow sly click. Wiggy was there.

—Then Jim came in and I was crying, and shouting at him what'd happened and he had to kill this fella, and the two of them just picked me up and brought me into the room—

And that was it, same as me. The men, one after another. Wiggy taking her to the bathroom. The Chinese girl cleaning the room. Blackheads and Wheezy arriving. Jim telling Chrissie to get dressed. The van. Nearly taking the fingers off herself trying to get the door open.

—I thought they'd kill me, she said.

And she cried for real now, nearly screaming with it.

I watched her do it. I felt kind of bored. I'd already been through it and I knew what'd happen now and it'd get worse. And how could I have helped, what could either of us have done.

21.

Chrissie wanted us to escape.

What'll happen to us, she said, how long will we be here? And I laughed at her. I couldn't help it. And she hit me and we fought on the floor til we both cried.

—We have to get out, she said. —We have to fucking get out—

I watched her, doing what I'd done weeks and a lifetime ago, checking locks and windows and looking out from behind the curtains. I said nothing.

The Twelfth weekend. Double bank holiday.

Busy busy busy.

Dublin, later. A weekend in a hotel.

I screamed once when it started, then I was scared the staff could hear and Blackheads would kill me. But then I thought the hotel staff were probably in on it like Wiggy Wanker had been in Belfast. I was right, a man later had the hotel name on his chest. Red threaded letters on a goldy beige shirt. The Montrose. I saw a brochure for it years later in the bus station and it was like being hit in the face.

Derry. Drogheda. Portrush. Loads of places too I didn't see street names or signs for, cos we were in the van and then in the middle of nowhere or on some estate.

And that time with the pool, like in a sports club. But I was on my own for that. And every time was like the first and it never stopped being sore.

22.

I'm crying. I'm letting on not to and Gemma is letting on not to see. The Housing Executive have accepted my new claim, they've agreed I'm nil income so they're going to pay housing benefit for me again. Not loads, not enough to cover the hostel, but Gemma says her manager's agreed they can use emergency funds to Make Up the Shortfall.

—Isn't it great, Lisa, isn't it great, Gemma says. —You can stay here now and in eleven weeks you'll get your dole money reinstated so it'll all be OK—

But. The new claim means I've had to declare myself homeless again. It means I have to start all over again, and all the waiting I've done so far is for nothing.

I have to get out by myself.

23.

Chrissie stopped talking about getting away. Mostly she mostly did, she'd still say it sometimes.

We were hardly ever on our own now there were two of us, men were in nearly all the time and if one of us was sleeping – well there was the other one. But on our own, sometimes she'd say it.

—We can do it, she'd say. —We need to get something sharp, and stab Blackheads and get the keys and run—

I'd say about the UVF and she'd say it'd be all right, we'd run far and they'd never find us.

I thought for half a second. We could get to Dublin, to England on the ferry. To Scotland from Larne maybe. They wouldn't find us in Scotland or England, they couldn't.

But we'd have to get to the ferry first, and we didn't know where it was. And we'd no money, hardly any food. I didn't have shoes.

—No, I said.

But I thought about it. In bed, when I was let alone for a bit, just to get out of my head for a minute.

There was nothing sharp in the flat, I'd looked. A knife for buttering toast and a plastic fork from a Chinese. Two cups, plastic, bright beakers like for kids. And then just the toaster, and what could we do with that, make Blackheads stick the knife in it?

Nothing in the living room, only the TV. No lamp bases or anything heavy to hit him on the head with. I looked again at the TV. I could lift it maybe, but probably not high enough to hit anyone with it—

The bathroom had no razors left in it, but Chrissie thought maybe when one of us was in the bath and Blackheads had brought a razor round and he was watching, the other one of us could sneak into the kitchen to look for more razors, maybe he brought them round in a pack. If we got one we could hold him hostage, get the keys. But I looked once when Chrissie was in the bath and there was nothing. Blackheads didn't even take his coat off.

Maybe the bog seat. Unscrew it and hit him with it. I couldn't remember in bed, but when I checked later it was plastic so it was no good. There was nothing else, unless I stabbed him in the eye with a toothbrush.

If we couldn't stab him, or hit him, or do anything to knock him out, there was nothing.

Chrissie was wrong. There was no way.

So I skipped that when I floated. I started with us on the street, running hard, knowing somehow no-one would chase.

But then there was the threesome. And my mind sort of snapped, and said I'll get out of here even if it's in a fucking box.

It's one I won't write about. Me and Chrissie and a man, a new one. Younger, a bit like Sean at the gulag.

—Which one? Blackheads said.

And the man said,

—Both of them.

Chrissie and me had to do stuff to each other.

I was so hot with shame after that I thought yeah, I really do want to die.

I checked the windows again. It wasn't about shouting for help now. It was about jumping. I was done, fucking, totally, fucking knackered.

But I knew there was no chance getting out through the window. It had to be the front door, we had to get out that way. Somehow.

—C'mon do it, I said, a couple of days later, when me and Chrissie could be in the same room.

She was delighted. I think she might've hugged me if it hadn't been for what'd happened two days before.

We talked over and over. For days.

Chrissie's idea was still to hit Blackheads over the head, then run. But that'd be too dodgy, I thought, we might not knock him out, and Wheezy or someone might be outside the flat. There was nothing to hit with anyway.

And then I was drifting one night, in bed half asleep. We couldn't get out by getting past Blackheads, so we'd have to somehow get out when he wasn't there. And cos we couldn't pick locks, someone would have to rescue us.

But how would the someone know we were there? We couldn't pull back the curtains and wave to the street, cos we couldn't open the window to shout out. We'd have to get rescued, properly rescued. Someone had to come, up to the flat, and take us away.

Rescue… How would we be rescued. Who rescued people?

It fizzed into my head. The fire brigade. The fire brigade rescued people.

We needed to start a fire.

24.

I thought maybe Chrissie would say wise the fuck up, we can't do that. But she said it was brilliant.

—How, but? she said. —How do we start a fire?

I knew how. We only needed a bit of paper, cos then we could set fire to it in the toaster. We used to do that in the gulag kitchen when we didn't have a light — we banged down the lever of the toaster, held a piece of paper to the glowing element, lit our smokes and dropped the flaming scrap into the sink. The staff used to crack up about it.

—Then we light something else with the bit of paper before it flames up too much, a bit of towel or something, and we run into the living room and set fire to the curtains—

The curtains were at the window, of course, so someone would see the fire from the street. They'd ring the fire brigade and we'd be rescued.

Chrissie said,

—What if no-one rings in time?

I shrugged.

I don't mean to be hard, making out to be tough or a hero. I just didn't give a flying fuck. The fire safety ads on TV said people died in house fires being Overcome By Smoke. If no-one came in time we'd just be Overcome By Smoke. It wouldn't even hurt.

And if we were rescued in time—

—We have to run once the firemen take their eyes off us, I said. —Cos if they get our names or take us to hospital, we'll be back at the gulag. And then we're fucked, cos Jim and Rocky'll find out in like a day—

—Yeah, she said.

She said, —When?

But then Blackheads was there, so we didn't talk for hours.

I looked for Chrissie. It was early in the morning, with light starting through the curtains. She was on the couch, sleeping. She woke up when she heard me.

—Tonight? I said, and she said yeah.

25.

It was riskier at night, cos there'd be more chance of men being in the flat. But people would see a fire better in the dark. We had to wait til we were alone and we never knew when that'd be.

It was nearly worse, once we decided. That day there were three men and I was sick after two. Chrissie cried all day after they left. We waited for dark. I thought it was what hell would be like, a last day going on and on and never getting away from it.

Dark was coming. We couldn't wait longer. Blackheads could come in any minute, he could be coming up the stairs right then.

I was sick again. I was shaking. I lay on the bathroom floor, cos the tiles were cool. C'mon leave it, I nearly said. Only we couldn't, cos then what?

I started to cry, big howls that ripped me.

But we had to do it.

Chrissie came to the bathroom to get me. My legs wouldn't work. Chrissie held me up but I think I held her up too. In the kitchen, the toaster was there, looking at us.

Where was the paper? We didn't know what to use, we thought maybe cardboard from a sandwich box. But Chrissie remembered the takeaway menus pushed through the letterbox. Most were shiny, paper that's good for roaches but not for burning. But one was proper paper. A pizza menu, red and green and white.

I took it. I squeezed the toaster lever down. Chrissie's Sugar Plum Fairy skirt lay on the counter.

Was Blackheads outside? Was he coming up the stairs?

I folded the menu like a fan. I held it to the fiery elements of the toaster. My hand shook so much Chrissie had to hold it still.

The paper curled. It caught and I had fire in my fist.

I thrust it at Chrissie's skirt.

The material went up right away. Too much, it was nearly eaten already—

Chrissie and me stared, freaking out. We hadn't said which of us would grab the skirt, who'd run to the curtains with it—

The skirt burned. I screamed and picked it up. It was roasting in my hands but I ran with it, right into the living room with the skin melting off my hands. I wanted to hold the material to the bottom of the curtains so they caught, but I couldn't hold it any more so I threw the skirt onto the carpet.

I didn't throw it far enough to reach the curtains. It wasn't heavy enough. It just started to burn the carpet, wisps of smoke and fire spreading on the cream.

I choked, cried. I fell on the carpet and I shoved the burning remains of Chrisse's Sugar Plum Fairy skirt to the end of the heavy brown curtains.

The flames licked one of the curtains. They caught. They caught fast. The curtain went up with a whoosh so fast and hard I felt it on my face.

Chrissie screamed. Or maybe it was me.

It was so fast!

—Open the other curtain! I screamed. —Open the fucking curtain!

But she screamed and cried, in hysterics. I was starting to go too, madness dancing on my mind's edge, cackling and wanting in.

If I let it I was dead. And now I knew I didn't want to be—

The curtain was half gone, roaring in flames. I yanked the other one open. I did it so hard it ripped off the rail. The carpet was on fire now and the second curtain caught at it and went up.

We'd thought we'd stay at the window once the curtains were open, going Halp! Halp! like Penelope Pitstop, and maybe coughing a bit until a fireman came up a ladder and lifted us out.

But it all happened too fast. I couldn't see—

There was black smoke now, and the flames were too hot, right to my feet—

I scrabbled back. I banged into Chrissie and she tumbled to the floor, over me—

A flame shot out, getting my sleeve, some trailing cheap seethrough shit Blackheads had bought.

On fire I was on fire—

I couldn't hear Chrissie screaming any more cos I was screaming too.

The flames roared in my head. I batted my arm on the carpet. I leapt up and ran, into the hall and I slammed shut the door of the living room cos that's what to do in a fire close the door but where's Chrissie I can't see her where's Chrissie—

I tried to scream her name, but there was no sound cos it was like flames in my throat.

I ran to the front door but of course it was locked it was always locked and the fire was in the hall now and I ran to the bathroom and I slammed the door and the handle blistered under my hands and maybe I'd fill the bath and get into it but that might boil me boil me alive and Overcome By Smoke was fucking bullshit, the fire brigade were lying bastards—

There was shouting, outside the bathroom door. Maybe it was a neighbour, maybe the fire burnt open the front door—

I wasn't going to see. I crouched down. Everything roared, I couldn't breathe—

The door burst open.

It wasn't Chrissie, the shape was too big. A fireman?

A voice, like from miles away.

—Fucking stupid wee cunts!

It was him. It was Blackheads.

26.

I still have a burn on my face. Not big, about the size of a finger, pressed there from my cheek down to my chin. More on my wrists. Lots on my palms and fingers. One on the back of my hand. The burns are smooth and shiny now, like coins under skin.

They took me to hospital.

They took me to hospital cos I ran out of the flat.

I was so fired up (ha) and panicked that I knocked Blackheads over (ha).

I leapt out of the bath at him, it felt like my head nearly brushed the ceiling. I knocked him over. I ran, down the hallway and out the open door and down the stairs.

I wrenched at the heavy iron door. Air I needed air—

The fire brigade was there. A fireman rushed over. I struggled in his arms cos if they took me to hospital Blackheads would find me. The fireman thought I was panicked cos of the fire and he held me tight so I couldn't get away.

Then, an ambulance and then a cool white bed.

27.

Debbie takes the first one. He's a regular, she says after.

—Breath that'd knock you out—

She makes a face. We laugh, but I'm shitting myself.

Not cos of what they'll do. There's fellas here looking after us. Two of them, Debbie's mates. They take the money and give us our half, they'll kick the shit out of anyone who fucks about.

But I'm still shitting myself. Cos I've fought notthinkingaboutit notthinkingaboutit notthinkingaboutit *for four years. Writing it down is different. The fellas from the bar were different. It's the difference between lying under a man heaving and gasping on me, and them hurting me, on purpose. I can't bring those memories back into real life, I can't.*

Three, that first night.

I don't want to write about it.

I cry after. Debbie says to wise up.

—Sure it's easy money, she says. —Better than them taking it for free.

I drift.

I think of my flat. Of being a vet's assistant. I'll have a dog and he'll skid on the warm rug, rushing to greet me.

28.

The peelers came to the hospital. There was a man one and a woman one.

There was no how are you feeling are you all right. They loomed over me. The man peeler said,

—How did the fire start, Lisa?

I said I didn't know.

—What were you doing in the flat?

It was a friend of Chrissie's flat, I said, we were staying there.

The woman peeler joined in then. She said who was the friend and I said I didn't know his real name but he was called Rocky.

They didn't believe me and they didn't give a fuck about showing it.

—We know you were there as a prostitute, the man peeler said. He said *prostitute* like you'd say *streak of shit*. He was disgusted by me, I could tell. Some little tramp with black fingernails and matted hair. He could hardly talk without giving me a dirty look.

When they left I waited til dark. I took my drip out and found my clothes in the locker beside my bed. I sneaked down the corridor and to the lift and to the ground floor and out. It was the same hospital they'd taken me and Nicola to years before. The Royal, one of the nurses said.

I'd no shoes and it hurt to move, but I ran. I didn't know where I was going but I ran.

I broke into an empty house. Normally I'd be chuffed at myself doing that, Lisa O'Neill ninja and housebreaker extraordinaire. I couldn't have done that eight months before, when I still lived with my ma and Paul. I couldn't even nick stuff properly. Now, I'd lived in a squat, and I'd been In Care, and—

notthinkingaboutthatnotthinkingaboutthatnow.

I stayed in the empty house about three days, I think. Maybe two, maybe five. There was a plastic sheet on the floor and I pulled it over me and I lay there. The burns scorched but the rest of me was cold and shivery.

I shook under the plastic. I waited. Maybe I'd die. I waited to see.

As long as Blackheads and Rocky and the UVF didn't find me I didn't care about anything.

29.

I get a hundred and twenty quid that first night with Debbie, cos there was four men (happy days it was thirty quid each and not twenty).

I do some counting. I can't get a place like Niall's now, cos I can't get his landlord's number. I don't know how to find other bedsits. So it'll have to be a flat. So I'll need more money, cos it's about three hundred a month for a one-bedroom flat. But I think, the Housing Executive won't pay for a place just for me, not if it's private rental—

I'll have to do what I'm doing, forever.

Again I think about jumping.

30.

I got caught nicking out of a supermarket.

I was on my own for ages, in the empty house. Maybe I'll write about it properly sometime, but it's blurry, all that time, I only remember bits.

After the fire, after days, when I stopped shivering, I got up from under the plastic sheet. All I remember is I was so thirsty. I'd still no shoes so I went out after dark. It was like something from a film, something like Terminator, me running from alley to alley and fence to fence, for food and clothes and the start of a life.

This could be my life, maybe. I was sick sometimes about Rocky, and Wiggy, and the B&B and the apartment – once I was sick in the street and everyone looked at me, and that's when I started *notthinkingaboutit*. But I was away from them now, and if I stayed away from everyone no-one could hurt me any more. Maybe – I didn't see how but maybe – I could get a job later and my own place.

I'd two big pieces of luck after the hospital. One was shoes, a pair of trainers outside a back door to air. They were a bit big for me but not too bad, not so anyone'd notice. So I could get into town now and look for money.

That was the second piece of luck, a purse in the market. A woman bought something and left her handbag open while she fussed with the shopping. So I reached in and lifted it, softly softly like Karen showed me and Nicola years ago in the squat.

I walked off fast, hands shaking as I looked in it. My first purse I ever stole had eighty quid in it, eightyfuckingquid, but this had seventeen and that was all right.

I bought a long sleeved top in a charity shop, cos I only had the burnt one and people kept looking at it and my arms and hands all burnt. Then I had fourteen quid left and I went to the knockoff food shop in North Street. I bought two stuffed bags of food for six quid, sandwiches and pies and crisps and chocolate, nothing that needed heating up.

I got into the empty house again, through the window. I thought I'd stay there. Until – until I didn't know what.

I lasted a while. A good while I think, some weeks. I took food from bins round the back of Tesco and Dunnes. It was all right food, just out of date. The back of the market was OK for stuff too at the end of the day when the traders packed up, but only fruit mostly cos the rest was raw fish and things in shells.

I took a blanket from a washing line. I nuck another purse. I found a coat in a charity shop for a fiver. It was cold now, coming into October.

I didn't know how I'd manage winter in the empty house, but I didn't know what else to do. I needed a squat like the one me and Nicola had stayed at months before, with other people to help nick stuff and with a SuperSer so I didn't freeze. But I didn't have a clue how to find one. Karen found us that time, she came up to us. I looked at scruffy girls, hard looking girls, in town. But no-one spoke to me.

I had nightmares. Every night, men on me, crushing me. When I woke up I'd think I was still in the apartment.

I cried most nights. I was on my own like I wanted but I think now I was lonely.

I got caught in the end.

I tried to nick a sausage roll from Tesco's. I was so cold, I hadn't eaten anything hot in months. I took the sausage roll from the deli counter in its warm bag and tried to walk out with it under my coat. Stupid, stupid again, I should've nuck money then bought the fucking sausage roll all legit. But I was so cold. I couldn't help it when I saw the sausage rolls all hot in their bags, I nearly felt one of them in my stomach.

The peelers who turned up about the sausage roll asked me my name and age, all hard and menacing the way they do over a tiny thing and they act like you've blown the place up. But it was obvious I was under eighteen, so then there was an Appropriate Adult, down in the copshop. Then social workers again. Another gulag. Belfast this time, miles away from where I'd met Rocky. I didn't know if that meant he'd find me or not.

They said I'd to attend school. I laughed at them.

I stayed for a week, then I left.

31.

I get the implant.

Debbie tells me about it so I go to the doctor. Hers has ran out she thinks but she doesn't care cos if she gets pregnant then she gets more points and she'll get a flat. I think about that for a couple of days but I decide no. I don't want a baby even for a flat. I don't want to be like my ma.

The hostel staff give me food from the donations cupboard, they give me tins and Cup a Soups. It's shit to take it cos I've got money, over three hundred quid now, hidden in my room in the ceiling under the tiles.

I can't tell them that, so I have to pretend I'm totally skint. Gemma buys me chips later, from her own money. I feel like shite. But I have to pretend.

The next time in the flat with Debbie, I stay the night. I don't want to go to the hostel cos they'll say I have to leave. But if they say it and I've the money to go, it'll be all right. Well, not all right, but better than a kick in the arse.

The hostel staff ring Debbie's mobile all night but she doesn't answer and then she lets the phone battery die.

February is cold and bitter and I've moved through it like underwater.

Four hundred and ninety quid now. I'm nearly there.

I can't afford anything yet, not in the area I want, but I look at the property section in the papers anyway. I'll figure out the next month's rent once I'm moved in. I'll have to leave the hostel without anyone seeing, cos otherwise the staff will want to know where the money's from. Gemma will know. I don't want to see her face, realising.

I'm nearly there.

I'm nearly there.

32.

I was in the Belfast gulag about a year and a half. Well, in and out, cos I kept leaving. I'd stay in winter and run in summer, and stay away for weeks. I'd go in winter sometimes too, a few days or a week here and there. I never met up with anyone and I never met fellas for money.

It'd be easy, I know where the girls stand in town. But I was *notthinkingaboutit*, so I didn't.

They gave up on school and got me a tutor and gave up on that too after I was sixteen. They knew they were only holding me til I was old enough to leave. I thought all the time about money and how to get my own place. When I was seventeen they said they could transfer me to the hostel, and I said OK, cos then I'd be on the housing list. I'd still run away whenever, I thought. But I didn't want to, not really. People left me alone more in an adult hostel, so I waited. I wanted to see what the housing people said.

I was vulnerable, everyone said so. So that should mean a flat. I didn't think I'd be here still two and a half years later. Yeah I'm vulnerable, but turns out loads of other people are too.

33.

I'm really, really tired.

It's the second of March.

I've over six hundred quid and I'm pretty much there. It's six weeks before my sanction ends from the dole. I'll ring about a flat, a bedsit in the paper. It's three hundred quid a month. It's a few streets from Niall. It's away from here.

Another letter arrives from the Housing Executive. What now, I think, cos I haven't done anything, but sometimes they send statements even though the rent goes straight to the hostel. So at first, I can't see it says what it does. I'm struck dumb.

Gemma sees. She snatches the letter from me, scared they've cut me off again. But then she reads it, fast. And she looks at me, and her eyes are shiny cos she's crying.

—Oh Lisa, she says. —The new build!

She's taking the piss. But she makes me look, she nearly pushes the paper into my face. And there it is.

I wasn't kicked off the first housing list. Maybe it's a mistake but I don't give a fuck.

I've reached the top of the list for the new build, the housing association one down by the old docks.

I'm getting one of the one-bed flats.

I'm getting one of them.

They're taking the piss. Someone's taking the piss.

Gemma shouts for the other staff. They rush in, probably thinking she's being murdered. She waves the letter.

—Lisa's got a flat! In the new build!

They crowd round. There's cheers and smiles and whoops. It can't be real. But I read the letter again, properly. It's real. I have a flat in the new build.

Gemma's crying. I'm crying too. It's been twelve years, craving own keys. It's been twelve years.

Belfast, April 2004

Gemma says will I be all right. Yeah, I say, nearly bouncing cos I want her to go.

She says call into the hostel anytime, she can give me advice on jobs or courses if I want and she wants to hear how writing down my story is going too. Yeah, I say again. I know she's being nice but I want her to go.

It's a Thursday in April.

It's my twentieth birthday next week.

I'm in my flat.

It took weeks to get the flat ready, it was a like a concrete box when I saw it, walls to be painted and carpets to go down. But I didn't care. I would've slept on the bare floor if they'd let me but they wouldn't.

I got a grant to furnish the flat. Gemma took me shopping. I got carpets for the living room and bedroom, grey and cheap cos I don't care about carpets. Paint for the walls, yellow for the living room and bedroom, white for the hall and bathroom. A couch and a fridge and a mini cooker from the Barnardos in Bridge Street.

A little table for the titchy kitchen. And a chair – only one.

Plates and saucepans, knives and forks. An iron and an ironing board. A duvet, sheets and pillows. A clock for the kitchen wall. A unit for the TV the hostel said I could keep. Clothes hangers for the built-in wardrobe. And a double bed that cost £120 and cleaned out the rest of the grant.

But I still have the six hundred quid. I earned it. So I'll have my yellow lamp, maybe even two, and I'll have posters and pictures too. I'll buy throws and cushions and a giant teddy bear. I'll do a massive food shop, everything a kitchen wants, but before I cook anything I'll eat pizza for a month and drink cider every day on my tiny balcony.

I'll finish writing my story. I might do a course. Gemma says I should, she says I'm Clearly Bright and also that I have Unfinished Potential. She says I should think about studying counselling. I don't know. Maybe I'll do acting, be in a play. I don't know. I've never had head room to think about it.

Gemma hugs me. I hug her. I'm nearly crying, but it's fifteen years building up. It's been fifteen years. *Please go, Gemma.*

She opens the front door.

—You take care of yourself now, she says again.

I say again I will.

I watch her walk down the hallway. Round the corner. I shake a bit, cos my big moment is coming up. Finally, I step back into the flat and I close the front door.

I close my own front door.

Help make a difference

Thanks so much for reading Take the Nights Back. I know a lot of you wanted to know what happened to Lisa after Taste the Bright Lights.

There are tough themes in this book, and I thought long and hard about putting Lisa through them. Like many readers, I wanted to give her a happy future and a happy ending. But I've worked with young women who have been in care and unfortunately those happy endings are very rare. Lisa would have needed a team of people around her, a lot of work to help her to trust them, and substantial counselling/therapy to help her ease the scars of her childhood. And government money just doesn't go to that.

So realistically, Lisa's sequel wasn't going to be a good one. But I feel very strongly that her story needed to be told regardless. Working with girls and young women like Lisa convinced me of that, and I've had lots of feedback on Taste the Bright Lights that the book has helped readers' daughters, granddaughters and younger sisters a little as they navigate growing up. That's all I wanted when writing these two books.

If you'd like to help Lisa's story get to the audience it should, I'd love if you could leave a review of this book. Any length is fine and I'd really appreciate it.

Enter the url bit.ly/tastethebrightlightssequel to go directly to your local Amazon page for the book.

You can also leave a review on my Goodreads and/or Bookbub pages: www.goodreads.com/laura_canning and https://www.bookbub.com/authors/laura-canning

Thank you so much.

Stay gold,

Laura

LAURA CANNING

TASTE THE BRIGHT LIGHTS

THE LISA DIARIES: BOOK 1

"ONE OF THE MOST AUTHENTIC TEENAGE VOICES YOU'LL EVER READ"

Also by Laura Canning

Taste the Bright Lights: The Lisa Diaries Book 1. The hard-hitting prequel to Take the Nights Back.

'Outstanding. Breathtaking. By god it deserves a hearing.'

When running from the cops is just the start of your problems.

A boot in the face. A broken nose. Blood on the classroom floor. And Lisa O'Neill and her best friend Nicola are fleeing from the police.

Lisa thinks she's finally free from her crappy home life. But sometimes the worst things are those on the road ahead... the ones you have no clue about.

When running to is worse than running from.

A blisteringly raw story of a teenage girl on the run from herself.

Buy Taste the Bright Lights at your local Amazon store:
bit.ly/airstriponepublications

About the author

Laura Canning grew up in Craigavon, Northern Ireland, in the 1980s and 1990s.

Since then she's travelled extensively and has worked as a proofreader, editor, ghostwriter, English teacher, and care worker in homeless and women's shelters. She's now based in London, living on a boat on the Thames and working as a full-time writer and editor.

Laura has an MA in creative writing, and a PGDip in magazine journalism from City University London. Her journalism has been published internationally and she was the lead writer for a multi award-winning travel website for ten years. She now writes fiction full time.

Extracurricular activities include reading, TV, travel and – lately – boxing: Laura fought (and won) her first fight for charity and will train for another fight as soon as possible after lockdown.